Blue Bloods

Blue Bloods

MELISSA DE LA CRUZ

HYPERION
NEW YORK

First Edition
3 5 7 9 10 8 6 4
Printed in the United States of America
This book is set in 12-point Baskerville.
Designed by Elizabeth Clark

Library of Congress Cataloging-in-Publication Data on file.
ISBN 0-7868-3892-2
Reinforced binding

Visit www.hyperionteens.com

This book is dedicated to my dad, Bert de la Cruz, true blue in every sense of the word, who has heroes' blood in his veins.

This book would not exist without the love, support, insight, and intelligence of my husband, Mike Johnston, to whom I owe everything.

The family was not simply the sum of the connections created by a large, extended set of relations . . . a family . . . was a name, a material and symbolic patrimony, and a form of stakeholding in America . . . "describing a total lineage, past, present and future."
—Eric Homberger, *Mrs. Astor's New York*

You can't push it underground
You can't stop it screaming out
How did it come to this?
You will suck the life out of me. . . .
—Muse, "Time Is Running Out"

One hundred and two people arrived on the Mayflower in November of 1620, but less than half lived to see the establishment of the Plymouth Colony the next year. While no one had died during the Mayflower's voyage, life after arrival was extremely difficult, especially for the young. Almost all of the lost were hardly sixteen years of age.

The staggering mortality rate was partly due to a harsh winter, as well as the fact that, while the men were out in the air, building homes and drinking fresh water, women and children were confined to the damp, crowded recesses of the ship, where disease could spread much more quickly. After the two-month voyage, they remained on the ship for an additional four months while the men built storehouses and living quarters on land. Young Puritans routinely cared for the sick, increasing their exposure to a vast array of illnesses, including a fatal affliction of the blood that historical documents called "consumption."

Myles Standish was elected governor of the colony in 1622 for thirty consecutive one-year terms. He and his wife Rose had fourteen children, a remarkable seven sets of twins. In an extraordinary turn of events, within a few years, the colony had doubled in size, with multiple births reported in all the surviving families.

—From *Death and Life in the Plymouth Colonies, 1620–1641* by Professor Lawrence Winslow Van Alen

Catherine Carver's Diary
21st of November, 1620
The Mayflower

It has been a difficult winter. The sea does not agree
with John, and we are always cold. Perhaps we
will find peace in this new land, although many
believe we have not left danger behind. Outside my
window, the coastline resembles Southampton, and
for that I am grateful. I will always long for
home, but our kind are no longer safe there. I myself
do not believe the rumors, but we must do as
instructed. It has always been our way. John and
I are traveling as husband and wife now. We are
planning on marrying soon. There are far too few of
us, and more are needed if we are to survive.
Perhaps things will change. Perhaps good fortune
will shine on us, and our situation will ameliorate.
The ship has anchored. We have landed. A new
world awaits!

—C.C

NEW YORK CITY

The Present

ONE

The Bank was a decrepit stone building at the tail
end of Houston Street, on the last divide between the
gritty East Village and the wilds of the Lower East Side.
Once the headquarters of the venerable Van Alen invest-
ment and brokerage house, it was an imposing, squat
presence, a paradigm of the beaux-arts style, with a classic
six-column façade and an intimidating row of "dentals"—
razor-sharp serrations on the pediment's surface. For many
years it stood on the corner of Houston and Essex, desolate,
empty, and abandoned, until one winter evening when an
eye-patch–wearing nightclub promoter chanced upon it after
polishing off a hot dog at Katz's Deli. He was looking for a
venue to showcase the new music his DJs were spinning—a
dark, haunted sound they were calling "Trance."

The pulsing music spilled out to the sidewalk, where
Schuyler Van Alen, a small, dark-haired fifteen-year-old girl,

whose bright blue eyes were ringed with dark kohl eye shadow, stood nervously at the back of the line in front of the club. She picked at her chipping black nail polish. "Do you really think we'll get in?" she asked.

"No sweat," her best friend, Oliver Hazard-Perry replied, cocking an eyebrow. "Dylan guaranteed a cakewalk. Besides, we can always point to the plaque over there. Your family built this place, remember?" He grinned.

"So what else is new?" Schuyler smirked, rolling her eyes. The island of Manhattan was linked inexorably to her family history, and as far as she could tell, she was related to the Frick Museum, the Van Wyck Expressway, and the Hayden Planetarium, give or take an institution (or major thoroughfare) or two. Not that it made any difference in her life. She barely had enough to cover the twenty-five dollar charge at the door.

Oliver affectionately swung an arm around her shoulders. "Stop worrying! You worry too much. This'll be fun, I promise."

"I wish Dylan had waited for us," Schuyler fretted, shivering in her long black cardigan with holes in each elbow. She'd found the sweater in a Manhattan Valley thrift store last week. It smelled like decay and stale rosewater perfume, and her skinny frame was lost in its voluminous folds. Schuyler always looked like she was drowning in fabric. The black sweater reached almost to her calves, and underneath she wore a sheer black T-shirt over a worn gray thermal undershirt; and under that, a long peasant skirt that swept the floor. Like a nineteenth century street urchin, her skirt hems were black with dirt from dragging on the sidewalks. She was wearing her favorite pair of black-and-white Jack Purcell sneakers, the ones with the duct-taped hole on the right toe. Her dark wavy hair was pulled back with a beaded scarf she'd found in her grandmother's closet.

Schuyler was startlingly pretty, with a sweet, heart-shaped face; a perfectly upturned nose; and soft, milky skin—but there was something almost insubstantial about her beauty. She looked like a Dresden doll in witch's clothing. Kids at the Duchesne School thought she dressed like a bag lady. It didn't help that she was painfully shy and kept to herself, because then they just thought she was stuck-up, which she wasn't. She was just quiet.

Oliver was tall and slim, with a fair, elfin face that was framed by a shag of brilliant chestnut hair. He had sharp cheekbones and sympathetic hazel eyes. He was wearing a severe military greatcoat over a flannel shirt and a pair of holey blue jeans. Of course, the flannel shirt was John Varvatos and the jeans from Citizens of Humanity. Oliver liked to play the part of disaffected youth, but he liked shopping in SoHo even more.

The two of them had been best friends ever since the second grade, when Schuyler's nanny forgot to pack her lunch one day, and Oliver had given her half of his lettuce and mayo sandwich. They finished each other's sentences and liked to read aloud from random pages of *Infinite Jest* when they were bored. Both were Duchesne legacy kids who traced their ancestry back to the *Mayflower*. Schuyler counted six U.S. presidents in her family tree alone. But even with their prestigious pedigrees, they didn't fit in at Duchesne. Oliver preferred museums to lacrosse, and Schuyler never cut her hair and wore things from consignment shops.

Dylan Ward was a new friend—a sad-faced boy with long lashes, smoldering eyes, and a tarnished reputation. Supposedly, he had a rap sheet and had just been sprung from military school. His grandfather had reportedly bribed Duchesne with funds for a new gym to let him enroll. He had immediately gravitated toward Schuyler and Oliver, recognizing their similar misfit status.

Schuyler sucked in her cheeks and felt a pit of anxiety forming in her stomach. They'd been so comfortable just hanging out in Oliver's room as usual, listening to music and flipping through the offerings on his TiVo; Oliver booting up another game of Vice City on the split screen, while she rifled through the pages of glossy magazines, fantasizing that she too, was lounging on a raft in Sardinia, dancing the flamenco in Madrid, or wandering pensively through the streets of Bombay.

"I'm not sure about this," she said, wishing they were back in his cozy room instead of shivering outside on the sidewalk, waiting to see if they would pass muster at the door.

"Don't be so negative," Oliver chastised. It had been his

idea to leave the comfort of his room to brave the New York nightlife, and he didn't want to regret it. "If you think we'll get in, we'll get in. It's all about confidence, trust me." Just then, his BlackBerry beeped. He pulled it out of his pocket and checked the screen. "It's Dylan. He's inside, he'll meet us by the windows on the second floor. Okay?"

"Do I really look all right?" she asked, feeling suddenly doubtful about her clothes.

"You look fine," he replied automatically. "You look great," he said, as his thumbs jabbed a reply on the plastic device.

"You're not even looking at me."

"I look at you every day." Oliver laughed, meeting her eye, then uncharacteristically blushing and looking away. His BlackBerry beeped again, and this time he excused himself, walking away to answer it.

Across the street, Schuyler saw a cab pull up to the curb, and a tall blond guy stepped out of it. Just as he emerged, another cab barreled down the street on the opposite side. It was swerving recklessly, and at first it looked like it would miss him, but at the last moment, the boy threw himself in its path and disappeared underneath its wheels. The taxicab never even stopped, just kept going as if nothing happened.

"Oh my God!" Schuyler screamed.

The guy had been hit—she was sure of it—he'd been run over—he was surely dead.

"Did you see that?" she asked, frantically looking around

for Oliver, who seemed to have disappeared. Schuyler ran across the street, fully expecting to see a dead body, but the boy was standing right in front of her, counting the change in his wallet. He slammed the door shut and sent his taxi on its way. He was whole and unhurt.

"You should be dead," she whispered.

"Excuse me?" he asked, a quizzical smile on his face.

Schuyler was a little taken aback—she recognized him from school. It was Jack Force. The famous Jack Force. One of those guys—head of the lacrosse team, lead in the school play, his term paper on shopping malls published in *Wired*, so handsome she couldn't even meet his eye.

Maybe she was dreaming things. Maybe she just *thought* she'd seen him dive in front of the cab. That had to be it. She was just tired.

"I didn't know you were a dazehead," she blurted awkwardly, meaning a Trance acolyte.

"I'm not, actually. I'm headed over there," he explained, motioning to the club next door to The Bank, where a very intoxicated rock star was steering several giggling groupies past the velvet rope.

Schuyler blushed. "Oh, I should have known."

He smiled at her kindly. "Why?"

"Why what?"

"Why apologize? How would you have known that? You read minds or something?" he asked.

"Maybe I do. And maybe it's an off day." She smiled. He

was flirting with her, and she was flirting back. Okay, so it was definitely just her imagination. He had totally not thrown himself in front of the cab.

She was surprised he was being so friendly. Most of the guys at Duchesne were so stuck-up, Schuyler didn't bother with them. They were all the same—with their Duck Head chinos and their guarded nonchalance, their bland jokes and their lacrosse field jackets. She'd never given Jack Force more than a fleeting thought—he was a junior, from the planet Popular; they might go to the same school but they hardly breathed the same air. And after all, his twin sister was the indomitable Mimi Force, whose one goal in life was to make everyone else's miserable. "On your way to a funeral?" "Who died and made you homeless?" were some of Mimi's unimaginative insults directed her way. Where was Mimi, anyway? Weren't the Force twins joined at the hip?

"Listen, you want to come in?" Jack asked, smiling and showing his even, straight teeth. "I'm a member."

Before she could respond, Oliver materialized at her side. Where had he come from? Schuyler wondered. And how did he keep doing that? Oliver demonstrated a keen ability to suddenly show up the minute you didn't want him there. "There you are, my dear," he said, with a hint of reproach.

Schuyler blinked. "Hey, Ollie. Do you know Jack?"

"Who doesn't?" Oliver replied, pointedly ignoring him. "Babe, you coming?" he demanded in a proprietary tone. "They're finally letting people in." He motioned to The

Bank, where a steady stream of black-clad teenagers were being herded through the fluted columns.

"I should go," she said apologetically.

"So soon?" Jack asked, his eyes dancing again.

"Not soon enough," Oliver added, smiling threateningly.

Jack shrugged. "See you around, Schuyler," he said, pulling up the collar on his tweed coat and walking in the opposite direction.

"Some people," Oliver complained, as they rejoined their line. He crossed his arms and looked annoyed.

Schuyler was silent, her heart fluttering in her chest.

Jack Force knew her name.

They inched forward, ever closer to the drag queen with the clipboard glaring imperiously behind the velvet rope. The Elvira clone sized up each group with a withering stare, but no one was turned away.

"Now, remember, if they give us any trouble, just be cool and think positive. You have to visualize us getting in, okay?" Oliver whispered fiercely.

Schuyler nodded. They walked forward, but their progress was interrupted by a bouncer holding up a big meaty paw. "IDs!" he barked.

With shaking fingers, Schuyler retrieved a driver's license with someone else's name—but her own picture—on its laminated surface. Oliver did the same. She bit her lip. She was *so* going to get caught and thrown in jail for this. But she remembered what Oliver had said. *Be cool. Confident. Think positive.*

The bouncer waved their IDs under an infrared machine, which didn't beep. He paused, frowning, and held their IDs up for inspection, giving the two of them a doubtful look.

Schuyler tried to project a calm she didn't feel, her heart beating fast underneath her thin layers. *Of course I look twenty-one. I've been here before. There is absolutely nothing wrong with that ID,* she thought.

The bouncer slid it under the machine again. The big man shook his head. "This isn't right," he muttered.

Oliver looked at Schuyler, his face pale. Schuyler thought she was going to faint. She had never been so nervous in her life. Minutes ticked by. People behind them in line made impatient noises.

Nothing wrong with that ID. Cool and confident. Cool and confident. She visualized the bouncer waving them through, the two of them entering the club. *LET US IN. LET US IN. LET US IN. JUST LET US IN!*

The bouncer looked up, startled, almost as if he'd heard her. It felt as though time had stopped. Then, just like that, he returned their cards and waved them forward, just as Schuyler had pictured.

Schuyler exhaled. She and Oliver exchanged a restrained look of glee.

They were inside.

Two

*R*ight next door to The Bank was a very different kind of Manhattan nightclub. It was the kind of nightclub that existed only once every decade—at a point in the social nexus when the gods of publicity, fashion, and celebrity converged to create a singularly spectacular environment. Following in the hallowed tradition of mid-'70s Studio 54, late-'80s Palladium, and early-'90s Moomba, Block 122 had entered an iconic realm that defined a movement, a lifestyle, a generation. A cocktail-combo clientele of the city's most beautiful, envied, notorious, and all-powerful citizens had christened it *their* place to be—their natural habitat, their watering hole—and since it was the twenty-first century, the era of super-exclusivity, they even paid astronomical membership dues for the privilege. *Anything* to keep out the hoi polloi. And inside this blessed sanctuary, at the most sought-after table, surrounded by a glittering assortment of underage models, post-pubescent movie stars, and the sons and daughters of boldfaced names, sat the most gorgeous girl in the history of New York City: Madeleine "Mimi" Force. Sixteen years old going on thirty-four, with a shot of Botox between the eyes to prove it.

Mimi was popularity personified. She had the golden-girl good looks and tanned, Pilates-toned limbs that came with the Queen Bee position—but she transcended the stereotype while embodying the essence of it. She had a size twenty-two waist and a size ten shoe. She ate junk food every day and never gained an ounce. She went to bed with all her makeup on and woke up with a clear, unblemished complexion, just like her conscience.

Mimi came to Block 122 every night, and Friday was no exception. She and Bliss Llewellyn, a tall, rangy Texan who'd recently transferred to Duchesne, had spent the afternoon primping for the evening's festivities. Or rather, Bliss had spent the afternoon sitting by the side of the bed making complimentary noises while Mimi tried on everything in her wardrobe. They'd settled on a sexy-but-in-an-off-beat-bohemian-way-with-straps-just-falling-off-the-shoulder-just-so-Marni camisole, a tiny denim Earnest Sewn miniskirt, and a sparkly Rick Owens cashmere wrap. Mimi liked to travel with an entourage, and in Bliss she'd found a suitable companion. She'd befriended Bliss solely at her father's request, since Senator Llewellyn was an important colleague. At first Mimi had chafed at the directive, but she changed her mind when she realized Bliss's equine good looks complemented and emphasized her own ethereal beauty. Mimi loved nothing more than a suitable backdrop. Leaning against the stuffed cushions, she glanced at Bliss approvingly.

"Cheers," Bliss said, clinking her glass against Mimi's, as if she'd read her mind.

"To us." Mimi nodded, chugging the last of her luminescent purple cocktail. It was her fifth of the evening, and yet she felt as sober as when she'd ordered the first one. It was depressing how much longer it took to get drunk now. Almost as if alcohol didn't have any effect on her bloodstream. The Committee had told her it would happen—she just hadn't wanted to believe it back then. Especially since she wasn't supposed to avail herself of the other, more potent alternative as often as she'd have liked. The Committee had too many rules. At this point they were practically running her life. She impatiently signaled to the waitress to bring another round, snapping her fingers so hard it almost shattered the glass coffee table in front of her.

What was the point of going out in New York if you couldn't even get a little buzzed? She stretched out her legs and lay them languidly across the couch, her feet resting on her twin brother's lap. Her date, the nineteen-year-old heir to a pharmaceutical fortune and a current investor in the nightclub, pretended not to notice. Although it would be hard to say if he was even conscious, as he was currently leaning on Mimi's shoulder and drooling.

"Quit it," Benjamin Force snapped, brusquely pushing her off. The two of them shared the same pale, platinum blond hair, the same creamy, translucent skin, the same hooded green eyes, and the same long, slender limbs. But they couldn't have been more different in temperament. Mimi was loquacious and playful, while Benjamin—nicknamed Blackjack in childhood because of his tantrums, and shortened to Jack in adolescence—was taciturn and observant.

Mimi and Jack were the only children of Charles Force, the sixty-year-old, steely-haired media magnate who owned an upstart television network, a cable news channel, a popular newspaper tabloid, several radio stations, and a successful publishing empire that made profits from autobiographies of World Wrestling Federation stars. His wife, the former Trinity Burden, was a doyenne of the New York society circuit, and chaired the most prestigious charity committees. She was instrumental in the foundation of The Committee, of which Jack and Mimi were junior members. The Forces lived in one of the most sought-after addresses in the city, a luxurious, well-appointed townhouse that covered an entire block across from the Metropolitan Museum of Art.

"Oh c'mon," Mimi pouted, immediately placing her feet back on her brother's lap. "I need to stretch my legs. They're so sore. Feel," she demanded, grabbing a sinewy calf and asking him to feel the muscle tense underneath. Strip Cardio was a bitch on the joints.

Jack frowned. "I said quit it," he murmured in his serious voice, and Mimi immediately retracted her tanned legs, tucking them beneath her butt and letting the undersoles of her four-inch Alaïa heels scrape against the white suede couch, leaving dirty scratch marks on the immaculate cushion.

"What's wrong with you?" Mimi asked. Her brother had arrived in a foul mood just a minute ago. "Thirsty?" she taunted. Her brother was such a party pooper lately. He hardly ever went to Committee meetings anymore, something their parents would freak out about if they ever found out. He wasn't dating anyone; he looked weak and spent, and he was undeniably cranky. Mimi wondered when the last time was that he had had any.

Jack shrugged and stood up. "I'm going out to get some air."

"Good idea," Bliss added, rising in a hurry. "I need a smoke," she explained apologetically, waving a pack of cigarettes in front of Mimi's face.

"Me too," Aggie Carondolet, another girl from Duchesne said. She was part of Mimi's crowd, and looked just like their leader, down to the $500-dollar highlights and sullen expression.

"You don't need my permission," Mimi replied in a bored voice, although the opposite was true. One didn't simply leave Mimi's presence—one was dismissed.

Aggie smirked, and Bliss smiled nervously, following Jack toward the back of the club.

Mimi shrugged. She never bothered to follow the rules, and tended to light up wherever and whenever she felt like it—the gossip columns once gleefully published the five-figure tally of her smoking fines. She watched the three of them leave, disappearing into the crush of bodies throwing themselves around the dance floor to obscene rap lyrics.

"I'm bored," she whined, finally paying attention to the guy who had hardly left her side all evening. They had been dating for all of two weeks, an eternity on the Mimi time line. "Make something happen."

"What do you have in mind?" he murmured groggily, licking her ear.

"Mmmm," she giggled, putting a hand underneath his chin and feeling his veins throb. Tempting. But maybe later, not here, not in public at least. Especially since she'd just had her fill of him yesterday . . . and it was against the rules . . . Human familiars were *not* to be abused, blah, blah, blah. They needed at least a forty-eight-hour recovery time . . . But oh, he smelled wonderful . . . a hint of Armani aftershave . . . and underneath . . . meaty and vital . . . and if she could just get one little taste . . . one little . . . bite . . . but The Committee met downstairs, right beneath Block 122. There could be several Wardens here, right now . . . watching . . . She could be caught. But would she? It was dark in the VIP room . . . Who would even notice in this crowd of self-involved narcissists?

But they would find out. Someone would tell them. It

was eerie how they knew so much about you—almost as if they were always there, watching, inside your head. So, maybe next time. She would let him recuperate from last night. She ruffled his hair. He was so cute—handsome and vulnerable, just the way she liked them. But for now, completely useless. "Excuse me for a second," she told him.

Mimi leaped from her seat so quickly that the cocktail waitress bringing a tray of lychee martinis to the table did a double take. The crew around the banquette blinked. They could have sworn she was sitting down just a second ago. Then in a flash, there she was: in the middle of the room, dancing with another boy—because for Mimi, there was always another boy, and then another and another, each one of them all too happy to dance with her—and it seemed like she danced for hours—her feet never even touching the ground—a dizzying, blond tornado in eight-hundred-dollar heels.

When she came back to the table, her face glowing with a transcendental light (or merely the effects of benefit high beam?), her beauty almost too painful to bear—she found her date sleeping, slumped over the edge of the table. A pity.

Mimi picked up her cell phone. She just realized that Bliss had never returned from that cigarette break.

THREE

She didn't fit in anywhere. She didn't know why. Was there ever anything so ridiculous as a sociophobic cheer-leader? Girls like her weren't supposed to have any problems. They were supposed to be perfect. But Bliss Llewellyn didn't feel very perfect. She felt odd and out of place. She watched as her so-called best friend, Mimi Force, needled her brother and ignored her date. A fairly typical evening around the Force twins—the two of them bickering one minute or being spookily affectionate the next—especially when they did that thing where they just looked into each other's eyes and you could tell they were talking to each other without speaking. Bliss avoided Mimi's gaze and tried to distract herself by laughing at the jokes the actor on her right was telling her, but nothing about the evening—not even the fact that they'd been given the best table in the house or that the Calvin Klein model on her left had asked for her number—made her feel any less miserable.

She'd felt that way in Houston, too. That somehow she was not all there. But in Texas, she could hide it more easily. In Texas, she had big curly hair and the best backflip on the squad. Everyone had known her since she was a "wee chile," and she'd always been the prettiest girl in her class. But then Daddy, who'd grown up in New York, moved them back to the city to run for the empty Senate seat and had won the election easily. Before she could do a rebel yell, she was living on the Upper East Side and enrolled at the Duchesne School.

Of course, Manhattan was nothing like Houston, and Bliss's big curly hair and backflips didn't mean a thing to anyone at her new school, which didn't even have a football team, much less mini-skirted cheerleaders. But on the other hand, she didn't expect to be such a hick. After all, she knew her way around a Neiman Marcus! She owned the same True Religion jeans and James Perse T-shirts as anyone else. But somehow, she'd arrived for the first day wearing a pastel Ralph Lauren sweater with a plaid Anna Sui kilt (in an effort to look more like the girls featured in the school catalog), with a honking white leather Chanel purse on a gold chain slung over her shoulder, only to find her classmates dressed down in grotty fisherman sweaters and distressed corduroys. No one wore pastel in Manhattan or rocked white Chanel (in the fall at least). Even that weirdo goth girl—Schuyler Van Alen—displayed a chic that Bliss didn't know how to match.

Bliss knew about the Jimmy, the Manolo, the Stella. She'd made note of Mischa Barton's wardrobe. But there was something about the way the New York girls put it together that made her look like a fashion freak who'd never cracked open a magazine. Then there was the whole deal with her accent—no one could understand her at first, and when she said "y'all" or "laaahke," they imitated her, none too kindly either.

For a moment, it looked as if Bliss would be consigned to live the rest of her academic life as a borderline social pariah, a home-schooled reject when she should have been a Mean Girl. That is, until the clouds parted—lightning struck—and a miracle occurred: the fabulous Mimi Force took her personally in hand. Mimi was a junior, a year older. She and her brother Jack were like, the Angelina Jolie and Brad Pitt of Duchesne, a couple who were not supposed to be a couple, but a couple nonetheless—and the ruling one at that. Mimi was the Orientation leader for new students, and she'd taken one look at Bliss—the pastel cardigan, the shiny bluchers, the awkward Scottish kilt, the quilted Chanel bag, and had said, "Love that outfit. It's so wrong, it's right."

And that was it.

Bliss was suddenly in the In-Group, which, it turned out, was just the same as the one back in Houston—jocky guys (but starting lacrosse and crew instead of football), uniformly pretty girls (but they were on the debate team and headed for the Ivy League)—with the same unwritten code to keep out newcomers. Bliss knew that it was only by Mimi's good graces that she'd managed to infiltrate the sacred stratum.

But it wasn't the social hierarchy of high school that was bothering Bliss. It wasn't even her blown-out-straight hair (which she would never let Mimi's stylist do to her again— she just didn't feel right without her curls), it was the fact that sometimes she didn't even feel like she knew who she was anymore. Ever since she had arrived in New York. She would walk by a building, or that old park by the river, and a feeling of déjà vu, but stronger—as if it were embedded in her own primal memory—would overwhelm her, and she would find herself shaking. When she walked into their apartment on East Seventy-seventh Street for the first time, she'd thought, "I'm home," and it wasn't because it was home . . . it was the feeling in her bones that she'd been there before, that she'd walked inside that same doorway before, that she'd danced across its marble floors in some not-so-distant past. "It used to have a fireplace," she thought, when she saw her room. Sure enough, when she mentioned it to the real estate agent, he'd told her it'd had a fireplace in 1819, but it had been boarded up for safety reasons. "Because someone died in there."

But the nightmares were the worst. Nightmares that left her screaming herself awake. Nightmares of running, nightmares of someone taking hold of her—as if she weren't in control—and she would wake up, shivering and cold, the sheets drenched with her sweat. Her parents assured her it was normal. Like it was a normal thing for a fifteen-year-old girl to wake up screaming so loudly her throat dried up and she choked on her own spit.

But now, at Block 122, Jack Force was standing up, and Bliss stood up too—excusing herself from Mimi's attention. She'd stood up on impulse, just to be moving, just to be doing something other than just being a spectator to the Show That Was Mimi, but when she'd said she needed a smoke, she found she really did. Aggie Carondolet, one of the Mimi clones, was already snaking her way outside. Bliss lost Jack halfway through the crowd, and she flashed the stamp on her right wrist to the guard, who had to let people out and back inside due to the draconian smoking laws in New York City. Bliss found it ironic that New Yorkers considered themselves so cosmopolitan—when in Houston, you could smoke any-where, even inside a beauty salon, while you were under the dryer; but in Manhattan, smokers were consigned to the margins and left to deal with the elements.

She pushed open the back door and found herself in an alleyway, a small dark corner between two buildings. The alley between Block 122 and The Bank was a petri dish of warring cultural allegiances—on one side, preening hipsters in tight, expensive, European clothes, tossing their bleached hair over zebra-print jackets; and on the other, a scraggly group of lost children in their tattered and pierced cloth-ing—but an uneasy truce existed between the two parties, an invisible line that neither group ever crossed. After all, they were all smokers here. She saw Aggie leaning against the wall, hanging out with a couple of models.

Bliss rooted in her hooded Marc Jacobs car coat (borrowed from Mimi, part of the makeover) for her cigarettes and tapped one out. She brought it to her lips, fumbling for the matches.

A hand extended from the darkness, offering a small, lit flame. From the other side of the alley. The first time someone had braved the divide.

"Thanks," Bliss said, leaning forward and inhaling, the cigarette glowing red at its tip. She looked up, exhaled, and through the smoke recognized the guy who'd offered it. Dylan Ward. A transfer—just like her—to the sophomore class from somewhere out of town. One of the odd-ones-out at Stepford-like Duchesne, where everyone had known everyone since nursery school and ballroom dancing lessons. Dylan looked handsome and dangerous in his customary beat-up black leather motorcycle jacket over a dirty T-shirt and stained jeans. It was rumored he'd been expelled from a succession of prep schools. His eyes glittered in the darkness. He flicked his Zippo closed, and she noticed his shy smile. There was something about him—something sad and broken and appealing . . . He looked exactly the way she felt, and he walked over to her side.

"Hey," he said.

"I'm Bliss," she said.

"Of course you are." He nodded.

FOUR

he Duchesne School was housed in the former Flood mansion on Madison Avenue and Ninety-first Street, on prep-school row, across from Dalton and next to Sacred Heart. It was the former home of Rose Elizabeth Flood, widow of Captain Armstrong Flood, who had founded the Flood Oil Company. Rose's three daughters were educated by Marguerite Duchesne, a Belgian governess, and when all three were lost during the unfortunate sinking of the SS *Endeavor* during an Atlantic crossing, a heartbroken Rose returned to the Midwest and bequeathed her home to Mademoiselle Duchesne to found her dream institution.

Little had been done to transform the home into a school: among the prerequisites of the behest was that all the original finishes and furniture were to be carefully maintained, which made entering the building akin to walking backward in time. A life-size John Singer Sargent portrait of the three Flood heiresses still hung above the marble staircase, welcoming visitors into the magnificent double-height entryway. A Baroque crystal chandelier hung in the glass-windowed ballroom that overlooked Central Park, and Chesterfield ottomans and antique reading desks were arranged in the foyer. The shiny brass sconces were now wired for electricity, and the creaky Pullman elevator still worked (although only faculty were allowed to use it). The attic, a charming garret room, was transformed into an art center, complete with a printing press and a lithograph machine, and the downstairs drawing rooms housed a fully equipped theater, gym, and cafeteria. Metal lockers now lined the fleur-de-lis wallpapered hallways, and the upper bedrooms housed the humanities classrooms. Generations of students swore that the ghost of Mrs. Duchesne haunted the third landing.

Photographs of each graduating class lined the hallway to the library. Since The Duchesne School was formerly an all-girls institution, the first class of 1869 showed a group of six dour-faced maidens in white ball gowns, their names gracefully etched in calligraphy. As the years progressed, the daguerreotypes of nineteenth-century debutantes gave way to the black-and-white photographs of bouffant-haired swans of the 1950s, to the cheerful addition of long-haired gentlemen in the mid-'60s, when Duchesne finally went coed, leading to bright color photographs of winsome young women and handsome young men from the current crop.

Because, really, not much changed. The girls still graduated in white tea dresses from Saks and white gloves from Bergdorf's, and were presented with garlands of twined ivy on their heads as well as the requisite bouquet of red roses along with their diplomas, while the boys wore proper morning suits, complete with pearl-tipped pins on their gray ascots.

The gray tartan uniforms were long gone, but at Duchesne, bad news still arrived in the form of a canceled first-period class, followed by an announcement made over rustling static on the antiquated sound system: "Emergency chapel meeting. All students asked to report to the chapel at once."

Schuyler met Oliver in the hallway outside Music Hum. They hadn't seen each other since Friday night. Neither of them had broached the subject of encountering Jack Force outside The Bank, which was highly unusual, since the two of them dissected every social situation they experienced down to the minute detail. There was a studied coolness in Oliver's tone when he saw Schuyler that morning. But Schuyler was oblivious to his aloofness—she ran up to him immediately and linked her arm in his.

"What's going on?" she asked, tucking her head against his shoulder.

"Hell if I know." He shrugged.

"You always know," Schuyler pressed.

"All right—but don't say anything." Oliver melted,

enjoying the feel of her hair against his neck. Schuyler was looking particularly pretty that day. She was wearing her long hair down for once, and she looked like a pixie in her oversized Navy peacoat, faded jeans, and broken-in black cowboy boots. He looked around nervously. "I think it has something to do with the crowd that was at Block 122 this weekend."

Schuyler raised her eyebrows. "Mimi and her people? Why? Are they getting expelled?"

"Maybe," Oliver said, savoring the thought.

Last year almost the entire crew team had been banished for illicit behavior on school grounds. To celebrate a win at the Head of the Charles, they had come back to school that evening and trashed the second-floor classrooms, leaving graffiti'd expletives on the walls and proof of their night— broken beer bottles, piles of cigarette stubs and several cocaine-laced dollar bills—to be found by the janitors the next morning. Parents petitioned the administration to change their decision (some thought expulsion too harsh, while others wanted nothing less than criminal charges filed). That the ringleader, a toothy Harvard-bound senior, was the Headmistress's nephew only added to the fire. (Harvard promptly recalled his admission, and the expelled coxswain was currently yelling himself hoarse at Duke.)

Somehow Schuyler didn't think that a simple case of bad behavior over the weekend was the reason the entire upper school was being called into the chapel that morning.

As there were only forty students in each class, the entire student body fit comfortably inside the room, taking their respective seats organized by grade: seniors and freshman in the front section separated by the aisle, juniors and sophomores respectively behind them.

The Dean of Students stood patiently by the podium in front of the altar. Schuyler and Oliver found Dylan in the back, at their usual perch. He had dark circles under his eyes, like he hadn't slept, and there was an ugly red stain on his button-down shirt and a hole in his black jeans. He was wearing his signature white silk Jimi Hendrix–style scarf around his neck. The other kids in the pew gave him a wide berth. He beckoned Schuyler and Oliver to his side.

"What's going on?" Schuyler asked, sliding into the pew.

Dylan shrugged, putting a finger to his lips.

Dean Cecile Molloy tapped the microphone. While she wasn't a Duchesne alum, like the headmistress, the head librarian, and almost the entire female faculty—and it was rumored that she'd been the recipient of a public school education—she had quickly acquired the velvet headband, knee-length corduroy skirts, and rounded vowels that marked the true Duchesne girl. Dean Molloy was a very adequate facsimile, and hence was very popular with the board of directors.

"Attention, please. Settle down, boys and girls. I have something very sad to share with you this morning." The dean inhaled sharply. "I am very sorry to inform you that one of our students, Aggie Carondolet, passed away this weekend."

There was a shocked silence, followed by a confused buzzing.

The dean cleared her throat. "Aggie had been a student at Duchesne since pre-kindergarten. There will be no classes tomorrow. Instead, there will be a funeral service in the chapel tomorrow morning. Everyone is invited to attend. Afterward, there will be a burial at Forest Hills in Queens, and a shuttle bus will be provided to take students who would like to attend, to the cemetery. We ask that you think of her family at this difficult time."

Another throat clearing.

"We have grief counselors on hand to assist those who need it. School will conclude at noon, your parents have already been informed of the early dismissal. After this meeting, please return to your second-period classes."

After a short invocation (Duchesne was nondenominational), and a devotion from the Book of Common Prayer, as well as a verse from the Koran and a passage from Khalil Gibran were read by the Head Boy and Head Girl, students streamed out with quiet trepidation, a low feeling of excitement mixed with nausea and real sympathy for the Carondolets. Nothing like this had ever happened at Duchesne before. Sure, they'd heard of other schools' problems—drunk driving accidents, child-molesting soccer coaches, senior boys date-raping freshmen girls, trench-coat-wearing freaks wielding machine guns and gunning down half the student body, but those happened at *other* schools—on television, in the suburbs, or in public schools, with their metal detectors and clear vinyl backpacks. Nothing terrible was ever allowed to happen at Duchesne. It was practically a rule.

The worst thing that could ever happen to a student at Duchesne would be a broken leg skiing in Aspen or a painful sunburn from St. Barth's over spring break. So the fact that Aggie Carondolet had *died*—in the city no less— just shy of her sixteenth birthday, was almost unfathomable.

Aggie Carondolet? Schuyler felt a twinge of sadness, but she didn't know Aggie, who had been one of the tall, pinched-looking blond girls who surrounded Mimi Force, like courtiers around their queen.

"You okay?" Oliver asked, squeezing Schuyler's shoulder. Schuyler nodded.

"Wow, that's heavy, man. I just saw her Friday night," Dylan said, shaking his head.

"You saw Aggie?" Schuyler asked. "Where?"

"Friday. At The Bank."

"Aggie Carondolet was at The Bank?" Schuyler asked skeptically. That made as much sense as Mimi Force being spotted shopping at J.C. Penney. "Are you sure?"

"Well, I mean, she wasn't technically at The Bank, but outside, you know, where everyone smokes downstairs, in the alley next to Block 122," Dylan explained.

"What happened to you?" Schuyler said. "We never saw you again after midnight."

"I, uh, met somebody," Dylan admitted, with a sheepish grin. "It's no big deal."

Schuyler nodded and didn't pry.

They walked out of the chapel, past Mimi Force, who was standing in the middle of a sympathetic circle of friends. "She'd just gone out for a smoke . . ." they overheard Mimi say, dabbing at her eyes. "Then she disappeared. . . . We still don't know how it happened."

"What are you looking at?" Mimi spat, noticing Schuyler staring at her.

"Nothing—I . . ."

Mimi flicked her hair over her shoulder and snorted in annoyance. Then she deliberately turned her back on the three of them and went back to reliving Friday night.

"Hey," Dylan said, passing the tall Texan girl in their class, who was part of the huddle. "Sorry about your friend." He put a light hand on her arm.

But Bliss didn't even acknowledge that she'd heard him.

Schuyler thought that was odd. How did Dylan know Bliss Llewellyn? The Texan girl was practically Mimi's best friend. And Mimi *despised* Dylan Ward. Schuyler had heard her calling him a "vagrant" and a "wastoid" to his face when he refused to give up his seat in the cafeteria. She and Oliver had warned him when he'd sat down, but he wouldn't listen. "But this is *our* table," Mimi had hissed, holding a tray that contained a paper plate of dry lettuce leaves surrounding an undercooked hamburger. Schuyler and Oliver had immediately grabbed their trays, but Dylan had refused to budge, which had instantly endeared him to them.

"It was a drug overdose," Dylan whispered, walking between Schuyler and Oliver.

"How do you know?" Oliver asked.

"It's the only thing that makes sense. She passed out at Block 122. What else could it be?"

Schuyler thought: aneurysm, heart attack, diabetic seizure. There were so many things that could cause a person's untimely demise. She'd read about them. She knew. She'd lost her father in her infancy, and her mother was stuck in a coma. Life was more fragile than anyone ever realized.

One minute, you could be getting a smoke in the alley on the Lower East Side with your friends, having drinks and dancing on tables in a popular night club. And the next minute, you could be dead.

FIVE

One of the best things about being Mimi Force was that nobody took you for granted. After the news of Aggie's death made the rounds, Mimi's popularity swelled to epic proportions—because now she wasn't just beautiful, she was vulnerable as well—she was *human*. It was like when Tom Cruise left Nicole Kidman, and suddenly Nicole Kidman stopped seeming like this icy, ruthless, career-minded Amazon and became just another dumped divorcée whom everyone could relate to. She'd even cried on *Oprah*. Aggie had been Mimi's best friend. Well, no, not exactly. Mimi had many best friends. It was the backbone of her popularity. Many people felt close to her, even though Mimi felt close to no one. But still, Aggie had been special to her. She'd grown up with her. Ice-skating at Wollman Rink, etiquette lessons at the Plaza, summers in Southampton. The Carondolets were an old New York family; her parents were friends with Mimi's parents. Their moms went to the same hairdresser at Henri Bendel. She was a true blue blood, like herself.

Mimi loved the attention, loved the fawning. She said all the right things, voicing her shock and grief with a halting voice. She dabbed her eyes without smudging her eyeliner. She recalled fondly how Aggie had lent her her favorite Rock and Republic jeans once. *And never even asked for them back!* Now that was a true friend.

After Chapel, Mimi and Jack were pulled aside by one of the runners, a scholarship kid who served as an errand boy for the Headmistress's office. "The Head wants to see you guys," they were told.

Inside the plush-carpeted office, the Head of Schools told them they could take the whole day off—no need to wait till noon. The Committee understood how close they were to Augusta. Mimi was elated. Even more special treatment! But Jack shook his head and explained that if it was all right with everyone, he was going to attend his second-period class.

Outside the administration corridor, the vast carpeted hallways were empty. Everyone else was in class. They were practically alone. Mimi reached out and smoothed her brother's collar, tracing her fingers on his sunburned neck. He flinched at her touch.

"What's gotten into you lately?" she asked impatiently.

"Don't, okay? Not here."

She didn't understand why he was so skittish. At some point, things would change. She would change. He knew that, but it was as if he couldn't accept it, or he wouldn't let himself accept it. Maybe it was all part of the process. Her father had made the history of the family very clear to them, and their part in it was set in stone. Jack didn't have a choice, whether he wanted it or not, and Mimi felt somewhat insulted at the way he was acting.

She looked at her brother—her twin, her other half. He was part of her soul. When they were little, it was like they were the same person. When she stubbed a toe, he cried. When he fell off the horse in Connecticut, her back ached in New York. She always knew what he was thinking, what he was feeling, and she loved him in a way that scared her. It consumed every inch of her being. But he'd been pulling away from her lately. He was distracted, distant. His mind was closed to hers. When she reached out to feel his presence, there was nothing. A blank slate. No, more like a muffling. A blanket over a stereo. He was tuning her out. Masking his thoughts. Asserting his independence from her. It was troubling, to say the least.

"It's like you don't even like me anymore," she pouted, lifting up her thick blond hair and letting it fall on her shoulders. She was wearing a black cotton sweater, rendered see-through underneath the fluorescent light of the hallway. She knew he could see the ivory lace of her Le Mystère bra through the thin weave.

Jack smiled a wry smile. "That's not possible. That would be like hating myself. And I'm not a masochist."

She shrugged her shoulders in slow motion, turning away and biting her lip.

He pulled her in for a hug, pressing his body against hers. They were the same height—their eyes at the same level. It was like looking into a mirror. "Be good," he said.

"Who are you and what have you done with my brother?" she cracked. But it was nice to be hugged, and she squeezed him back tightly. Now, that was more like it.

"I'm scared, Jack," she whispered. They'd been there, that night, with Aggie. Aggie shouldn't be dead. Aggie couldn't be dead. It just couldn't be true. It was impossible. *In every sense of the word.* But they'd seen Aggie's body at the morgue, that cold gray morning. She and Jack had been the ones to identify the body. Mimi's cell number was the first entry in Aggie's phone. They'd held her lifeless hands. They'd seen her face, the frozen scream. Much worse, they'd seen the marks on her neck. Unthinkable! Ridiculous, even. It simply didn't add up. It was as if the world had been turned upside down. It was against everything they'd been told. She couldn't even begin to make it comprehensible.

"It's a joke, right?"

"No joke." Jack shook his head.

"She's not just cycling early?" Mimi asked, hoping against hope that they'd found some reasonable explanation for all this. There had to be one. Things like this simply didn't happen. Not to them.

"No. They've done the tests. Worse. The blood—it's gone."

Mimi felt a chill up her spine. It was as if something had

skittered across her grave. "What do you mean it's gone?" she gasped.

"She was drained."

"You mean . . ."

"Full consumption." Jack nodded.

Mimi recoiled from his embrace. "You're joking. You have to be. It's just not—*possible*." That word again. That word that popped up all weekend, Saturday morning, when the call came: repeated by their parents, the Elders, the Wardens, everybody. What happened to Aggie just wasn't possible. That much they all agreed on. Mimi walked toward an open window, stepped into the sunlight, and gloried in the way it tickled her skin. *Nothing could hurt them.*

"They've called a conclave. The letters went out today."

"Already? But they haven't even begun to change yet," Mimi protested. "Isn't that against the rules?"

"Emergency situation. Everyone has to be warned. Even the premature."

Mimi sighed. "I suppose." She'd rather liked being one of the youngest. She didn't like knowing her novel status would soon be supplanted by a new batch.

"I'm going to class. Where are you going?" he asked, tucking his shirt into his pants, a futile move since when he reached for his leather satchel, the motion pulled his shirt-tails out again.

"To Barneys," she replied, putting on her sunglasses. "I have nothing to wear to the funeral."

chuyler's second-period class was ethics, a multi-year class open to sophomores and juniors completing their diversity studies requirements. Their teacher, Mr. Orion, a curly-haired Brown graduate with a droopy mustache, small, wire-rimmed glasses, a long Cyrano nose, and a penchant for wearing oversized baggy sweaters that hung off his scarecrowlike frame, sat in the middle of the room, leading the discussion.

She found a seat near the window, pulling up her chair to the circle around Mr. Orion. There were only ten people, the standard class size. Schuyler couldn't help but notice that Jack Force wasn't in his usual seat. She'd never said a word to him all semester, and she wondered if he would even remember saying hello to her on Friday night.

"Did anyone here know Aggie well?" Mr. Orion asked, even though it was an irrelevant question. Duchesne was the kind of place that, years after graduation, if you bumped into an alum at an airport, or walking around Centre Pompidou, or downtown at Max Fish, you would immediately buy them a drink and ask about their family, because even if you had never exchanged a word while at the school, you knew almost everything about them, down to the intimate details.

"Anyone?" Mr. Orion asked again.

Bliss Llewellyn cautiously raised her hand. "I did," she said timidly.

"Do you want to share some memories of her?"

Bliss put her hand down, her face red. Memories of Aggie? What did she really know about her? She knew that she liked clothes, and shopping, and her tiny little lapdog,

Snow White. It was a Chihuahua, like Bliss's, and Aggie had liked to dress her up in silly little outfits. The dog even had a mink sweater that matched Aggie's. That was as much as Bliss could recall. Who ever really knows anybody? And anyway, Aggie was really Mimi's friend.

Bliss thought back on that fateful night. She'd ended up talking to Dylan for what seemed like ages in that back alley. When they'd smoked every last cigarette they had between the two of them, he'd finally gone back to The Bank, and she'd reluctantly returned to Block 122 and Mimi's demands. Aggie wasn't at the table when she got back, and Bliss hadn't seen her for the rest of the evening.

From the Force twins, Bliss knew the basics—they'd found Aggie in "the Land of Nod"—the back room where the club hid druggies who'd passed out—a dirty little secret that Block 122 had successfully kept out of the tabloids, with hefty bribes to cops and gossip columnists alike. Most of the time patrons who passed out woke up hours later just a little worse for wear, with a great anecdote to tell their friends— "And I woke up in this closet, man! What a long strange trip, right?" and were sent home (mostly) intact.

But something had gone wrong on Friday night. They hadn't been able to revive Aggie. And when "the ambulance" (the owner's SUV) had deposited her at the St. Vincent's ER—Aggie was already dead. Drug overdose, everyone assumed. She'd been found in the closet, after all. What did you expect? Except Bliss knew that Aggie didn't touch drugs. Like Mimi's, her vices of choice were tanning salons and cigarettes. Drugs were looked down upon in Mimi's circle. "I don't need anything to get high. I'm high on life," Mimi liked to crow.

"She was . . . sweet," Bliss offered. "She really loved her little dog."

"I had a parrot once." A red-eyed sophomore nodded. She'd been the one who'd handed Mimi tissues in the hallway. "When she died, it was like losing a part of myself."

And just like that, Augusta "Aggie" Carondolet's death went from a tragedy to a mere springboard for an earnest discussion about how pets were people too, where to find pet cemeteries in the city, and whether cloning your pet was the right ethical choice.

Schuyler could barely disguise her contempt. She liked Mr. Orion, liked his shaggy-dog laid-back approach to life, but she was disgusted by the way he let her peers turn something real—the death of someone they knew, someone hardly sixteen years old—a girl they'd all seen sunbathing in the cortile, powering squash returns in the lower court gyms, or hoovering brownies at the bake sale (like all popular Duchesne girls, Aggie had a love affair with food that was out of proportion to her super-skinny appearance)—into a trivial matter, a stepping-stone to talk about everyone else's neuroses.

The door opened, and everyone looked up to see a red-faced Jack Force enter the room. He passed his late form to Mr. Orion, who waved it away. "Sit down, Jack."

Jack walked purposefully across the room to the only remaining empty seat in the classroom—next to Schuyler. He looked tired, and a little rumpled in his creased polo with the shirttails hanging out and baggy wool pants. A slight electric charge went through Schuyler's body, a prickly and not unpleasant sensation. What had changed? She'd sat next to him before, and he was always invisible to her, until now. He didn't meet her eye, and she was too frightened and self-conscious to look at him. It was odd to think they were both there that evening. So close to where Aggie had died.

But now another Mimi disciple was prattling about her

hamster, who'd starved to death when they went on vacation. "I just loved Bobo so much," she sobbed into a handkerchief as the rest of the class voiced their sympathy. Tales of the demise of a similarly beloved lizard, canary, and rabbit were next on deck.

Schuyler rolled her eyes and doodled in the margins of her notebook. It was her way of zoning out from the world. When she couldn't take it anymore—her spoiled classmates' navel-gazing rants, endless math lectures, the yawn-inducing properties of single-cell division—she retreated into pen and paper. She'd always loved to draw. Anime girls and saucer-eyed boys. Dragons. Ghosts. Shoes. She was absentmindedly sketching Jack's profile when a hand reached out and scrawled a note on top of her page.

She looked up, startled, instinctively covering her drawing.

Jack Force nodded somberly at her, tapping on her notebook with a pencil, directing her gaze to the words he'd written.

Aggie didn't die of an overdose. Aggie was murdered.

gleaming Rolls-Royce Silver Shadow was waiting in front of the Duchesne gates when Bliss emerged. She felt slightly embarrassed, like she always did when she saw the car. She saw her half sister, Jordan, who was eleven and in the sixth grade, waiting for her. They had let the lower form out early too, even though they hardly knew Aggie.

The door to the Rolls opened, and a pair of long legs stepped out of the car. Bliss's stepmother, the former BobiAnne Shepherd, wearing a tight pink velour tracksuit with the zipper pulled down to reveal her ample bosom, and high-heeled Gucci clogs, began looking frantically around the clustered students.

Bliss wished, not for the first time, that her stepmother would let her take a cab or walk home like every other kid at Duchesne. The Rolls, the Juicy, the eleven-carat diamond, it was all so Texas. Bliss had learned, from her two months in Manhattan, that it was all about stealth wealth. The richest kids in class wore Old Navy and were on strict allowances. If they needed a car, their parents made sure it was a sleek and unobtrusive black Town Car. Even Mimi took cabs. Flashy displays of status and affluence were looked down upon. Of course, these were also the same kids who wore pre-stained jeans and unraveling sweaters from precious SoHo boutiques that charged in the five figures. It was all right to *look* poor, but actually *being* poor was completely inexcusable.

At first, everyone at school thought Bliss was a scholarship kid, with her fake-looking Chanel bag and her too-shiny shoes. But the appearance of the Silver Shadow Rolls every afternoon soon put an end to that rumor. The Llewellyns were loaded, all right, but in a vulgar, cartoonish, laughable fashion, which was almost as bad as having no money, but not quite.

"Darlings!" BobiAnne trilled, her voice carrying down the block. "I was so worried!" She gathered her daughter and her stepdaughter in her skinny arms, pressing her powdered cheek against theirs. She smelled like calcified perfume—sweet and chalky. Bliss's real mother had died when she was born, and her father never talked about her. Bliss had no memory of her mother. When she was three, her father had married BobiAnne, and they'd had Jordan soon after.

"Stop it, BobiAnne," Bliss complained. "We're fine. We're not the ones who were killed."

Killed. Now, why had she said that? Aggie's death was an accident. A drug overdose. But the word had come out naturally, without her even thinking about it. Why?

"I do wish you'd call me Mama, darlin'. I know, I know. I heard. The poor Carondolet girl. Her mother is in shock, the poor thing. Get in, get in."

Bliss followed her sister inside the car. Jordan was stoic as usual, taking her mother's histrionic ministrations with a studied indifference. Her sister couldn't have been more dissimilar to her. Whereas Bliss was tall and willowy, Jordan was short and stocky. Bliss was strikingly beautiful, but Jordan was so plain she was almost homely, a fact that BobiAnne never failed to point out. "As different as a swan from a water buffalo!" she lamented. BobiAnne was always trying to put Jordan on some kind of diet and admonishing her for her lack of interest in fashion or a "beauty regimen" while praising Bliss's looks to the heavens, which aggravated Bliss even more.

"You girls are not to go out anymore without a chaperone. You especially, Bliss, no more sneaking out with Mimi Force to god knows where. You're to be home every night by nine." BobiAnne said, nervously gnawing on her thumbnail.

Bliss rolled her eyes. So now just because some girl died at a nightclub she had some kind of curfew? When did her stepmother even care about stuff like this? Bliss had been going to parties since seventh grade. She'd had her first taste of alcohol then, and had gotten stupid-drunk at the fairgrounds that year; her friend's older sister had had to come and pick her up after she'd vomited and passed out in the haystack behind the Ferris Wheel.

"Your father insists," BobiAnne said anxiously. "Now, don't y'all give me any more trouble about it, y'hear?"

The Rolls pulled away from the Duchesne gates, drove down the length of the block, and made a U-turn to stop in front of the Llewellyn's apartment building right across the street.

They exited the car and walked into a palatial apartment building. The Anthetum was one of the oldest and most prestigious addresses in the city. The Llewellyn abode was a triplex penthouse on the top floor. BobiAnne had commissioned several interior designers to decorate the place, and had even given the apartment a grand name, *Penthouse des Rêves* (Penthouse of Dreams) even though all the French she knew could fit in a dress tag (*Dry Clean Seulement*). Each room in the apartment was decorated in flamboyant, peacock fashion, and no expense had been spared, from the floor-standing eighteen-carat gold candlelabras in the dining room to the diamond-encrusted soap dishes in the powder room.

There was the "Versace" sitting room, filled with the dead designer's antiques that BobiAnne had scooped up at the auction, filled to the brim with sunburst mirrors, gold gilt china cabinets, and bombastic Italian nude sculpture. Another room was the "Bali" room, with wall-to-wall mahogany armoires, rough wooden benches, and bamboo bird cages. Every item in the room was an authentic, extremely rare and expensive South Asian artifact, but because there were so many of them, the overall effect was that of a fire sale at Pier 1 Imports. There was even a "Cinderella" room, modeled after the exhibit at Disney World—complete with a tiara-wearing mannequin in a dress held up by two fiberglass birds attached to the ceiling.

Bliss thought *Penthouse de Crap* would be more fitting.

Her stepmother was particularly agitated that afternoon. Bliss had never seen her so nervous. BobiAnne didn't even flinch when Bliss trailed dirty footsteps on the immaculate carpet.

"Before I forget, this came for you today." Her stepmother handed Bliss an oversize white linen envelope. It had an impressive heft and weight to it, like a wedding announcement. Bliss opened it, finding a thick embossed card inside. It was an invitation to join the New York Blood Bank Committee. One of the oldest charities in New York, it was also the most prestigious; only the children of the most socially prominent families were invited to join as junior members. At Duchesne, it was simply called "The Committee." Everyone who was anyone in school was in The Committee; being a member elevated you to a level of the social stratosphere that was so lofty, mere mortals could only aspire to, but never reach its heights.

Captains of all the school teams were on The

Committee, as were the editors of the newspaper and yearbook, but it wasn't an honor society, since rich kids like Mimi Force, who weren't active in any school activities but whose parents were influential New Yorkers, made up the bulk of the membership. It was snobby, cliquey, and exclusive to the extreme; membership comprised of only kids from the top private schools. The Committee had never even released a full list of its members—if you were on the outside, you could only guess if someone was in it, and only a clue, like a Committee ring, a gold serpent around a cross, worn by a member, would give it away.

Bliss had been under the impression they weren't inducting new members until the spring, but the packet informed her the first meeting was for the following Monday, at the Jefferson Room at Duchesne.

"Why would I want to join a charity committee?" she asked, thinking it was all so silly. All that hoopla over fundraising and party-planning. She was sure Dylan would find it ridiculous. Not that she cared what Dylan thought. She still didn't know how she felt about him—she felt awful about not even saying hello when he'd tapped her on the shoulder earlier. But Mimi's watchful eyes were upon her, and Bliss just hadn't felt brave enough to give any indication that they were friends. Were they friends? They were certainly friendly Friday night.

"You don't join. You've been chosen," BobiAnne said.

Bliss nodded. "Do I have to?"

BobiAnne was adamant. "It would make your father and I very happy."

Later in the evening, Jordan knocked on Bliss's bedroom door. "Where were you on Friday night?" she asked, her chubby fingers resting on the doorknob, leaving sticky fingerprints on its gold plate. Jordan's dark eyes peered at her in an unnerving fashion.

Bliss shook her head. Her little sister was so strange. She was so alien to Bliss. When they were younger, Jordan had followed her everywhere like a lost puppy, and continually wondered why she didn't have curly hair like her sister, fair skin like her sister, and blue eyes like her sister. They used to be friends. But things had changed in the past year. Jordan had become secretive and shy around Bliss. It had been ages since Jordan had asked Bliss to braid her hair.

"At Block 122, you know, that private club all the celebs go to. It was in *US Weekly* last week," Bliss replied. "Why, who wants to know?" She was sitting on her princess bed, Committee papers spread out on the duvet. For a charity committee, there were an endless number of forms to be filled out, including a statement of acceptance, that included a commitment of two hours every Monday night.

"That's where she died, isn't it?" Jordan said darkly.

"Yeah." Bliss nodded, without looking up.

"You know who did it, don't you?" Jordan said. "You were there."

"What do you mean?" Bliss asked, finally putting down the papers.

Jordan shook her head. "You *know*."

"Actually, I have no idea what you're talking about. Didn't you get the 411? It was an overdose. Now, get lost, puke-face," Bliss said, throwing a pillow at the door.

What was Jordan talking about? What did she know? Why had her stepmother been so affected by Aggie's death? And what was the big deal about joining some charity committee?

She called Mimi. She knew Mimi was on The Committee, and Bliss wanted to make sure she was going to be at the meeting.

Catherine Carver's Diary
25th of November, 1620
Plymouth, Massachusetts

Tonight we celebrated our safe journey into our new home. We have joyful news—the people of this new land have welcomed us with open arms and many gifts. They brought wild game, a large bird that could feed an army, a bounty of vegetables, and maize. It is a new beginning for us, and we are heartened by the sight of the verdant land, the vast virgin acres where we will make our settlement. All our dreams have been realized. This is what we left our homes for—so that the children may grow up safe and whole.

—C.C.

hen school let out, Schuyler caught the crosstown bus at Ninety-sixth Street, sliding her white student MetroCard in the slot and finding an empty seat next to a harassed-looking mother with a double stroller. Schuyler was one of the few students at Duchesne who took public transportation.

The bus slowly lumbered across the avenues, past a host of specialty boutiques on Madison, including the unapologetically-named "Prince and Princess" that catered to the elite under-twelve set—French-smocked cotton dresses for girls and Barbour coats for boys; pharmacies that stocked five-hundred-dollar boar's-hair brushes; and tiny antique shops that sold arcana such as mapmaking equipment and fourteenth-century feather quills. Then it was through the Central Park greenery to the west side of town, toward Broadway, a change of neighborhood and scenery—Chino-

Latino restaurants, less snooty retail shops—then finally a steep right up Riverside Drive.

She had meant to ask Jack what he'd meant by his note, but she hadn't been able to catch him after class. Jack Force, who had never even paid attention to her before? First he knows her name, now he's writing her notes? Why would he tell her Aggie Carondolet was murdered? It had to be some kind of joke. He was playing with her, scaring her, most likely. She shook her head in irritation. It didn't make sense. And even if Jack Force had some overheated *Law and Order*-type insight into the case, why was he sharing it with her? They barely knew each other.

At 100th street, she dinged the yellow tape and stepped lightly out the automatic doors to the still-sunny afternoon. She walked up one block toward the steps carved into the landscaped terraces that separated the traffic and led directly to her front door.

Riverside Drive was a scenic Parisian-style boulevard on the westernmost side of upper Manhattan: a grand serpentine route dotted with stately Italian Renaissance mansions and majestic Art Deco apartment buildings. It was here that the Van Alens had decamped in the turn of the last century from their lower Fifth Avenue abode. Once the most powerful and influential family in New York City, the Van Alens had founded many of the city's universities and cultural institutions, but their wealth and prestige had been in decline for decades. One of their last remaining holdings was the imposing French-style palace on the corner of leafy 101st and Riverside Drive that Schuyler called home. Made of beautiful gray stone, it had a wrought-iron door and gargoyles standing guard at the balcony level.

But unlike the sparkling refurbished townhouses that surrounded it, the house badly needed a new roof, tiles, and a coat of paint.

Schuyler rang the doorbell.

"I know, I'm sorry, Hattie, I forgot my keys again," she apologized to their housekeeper, who had been with the family ever since Schuyler could remember.

The white-haired Polish woman in an old-fashioned maid's uniform only grunted.

Schuyler followed her through the creaking double door and tiptoed across the great hall, which was dark and musty with Persian rugs (so old and rare, but covered in a layer of dust). There was never any light in the room because, even though the house had several large bay windows that overlooked the Hudson River, heavy velvet curtains always covered the views. Traces of the family's former largesse were in evidence, from the original Heppelwhite chairs to the massive Chippendale tables, but the house was too hot in the summer and too drafty in the winter, without the benefit of central air. Unlike the Llewellyn's penthouse, where everything was either a pricey reproduction or an antique bought at Christie's, every piece of furniture in the Van Alen home was original and handed down from earlier generations.

Most of the home's seven bedrooms were locked and unused, and draped fabric covered most of the heirloom pieces. Schuyler always thought it was a little like living in a creaky old museum. Her bedroom was on the second floor—a small room she'd rebelliously painted a bright Mountain Dew yellow, to contrast the dark tapestries and stuffiness of the rest of the house.

She whistled for Beauty, and a friendly, gorgeous bloodhound ran to her side. "Good girl, good girl," she said, kneeling down and hugging the happy creature, letting it lick her face. No matter how bad a day she'd had, Beauty always made it better. The beautiful animal had followed her home from school one day last year. The dog was a purebred, with a glossy dark coat that matched Schuyler's blue-black hair. Schuyler had been sure her owners would come looking for her, and she had put up "Found Pet" signs in the neighborhood. But no one came to claim Beauty, and after a while, Schuyler stopped trying to find her rightful owner.

The two of them loped up the stairs. Schuyler walked inside her room and shut the door behind her dog.

"Home so soon?"

Schuyler nearly jumped out of her coat. Beauty barked, then wagged her tail, galloping joyfully toward the intruder. Schuyler turned to find her grandmother sitting on the bed with a stern expression. Cordelia Van Alen was a small, birdlike woman—it was easy to see where Schuyler got her delicate frame and her deep-set eyes, although Cordelia usually dismissed remarks about family resemblance. Cordelia's eyes were blue and bright, and they stared intensely at her granddaughter.

"Cordelia, I didn't see you," Schuyler explained.

Schuyler's grandmother had forbidden her to call her Grandmother, or Grandma, or as she heard some children call them, Nana. It would be nice to have a Nana, a warm and chubby maternal figure, whose very name spelled love and homemade chocolate chip cookies. But instead, all Schuyler had was Cordelia. A still-beautiful, elegant woman, who looked to be in her eighties or nineties, Schuyler never knew which. Some days, Cordelia looked young enough to be in her fifties (or forties even, if Schuyler was being honest with herself). Cordelia sat ramrod straight, dressed in a black cashmere cardigan and flowing jersey pants, her legs crossed delicately at the ankles. On her feet were black Chanel ballet slippers.

All throughout Schuyler's childhood, Cordelia had been a presence. Not a parental, or even an affectionate one, but a presence nonetheless. It was Cordelia who had changed Schuyler's birth certificate so that her last name was her mother's and not her father's. It was Cordelia who had enrolled her at the Duchesne School. Cordelia who signed her permission slips, monitored her report cards, and provided her with a paltry allowance.

"School let out early," Schuyler said. "Aggie Carondolet died."

"I know." Cordelia's face changed. A flash of emotion

flickered across the stern features—fear, anxiety, concern, even?

"Are you all right?"

Schuyler nodded. She barely even knew Aggie. Sure, they'd been going to the same school for more than a decade, but it didn't mean they were friends.

"I've got homework to do." Schuyler said, as she unbuttoned her coat and shook off her sweater, peeling each layer of clothing until she stood in front of her grandmother in a thin white tanktop and black leggings.

Schuyler was half afraid of her grandmother, but had grown to love her even though Cordelia never showed any inclination of reciprocating the sentiment. The most palpable emotion Schuyler could detect was a grudging tolerance. Her grandmother tolerated her. She didn't approve of her, but she tolerated her.

"Your marks are getting worse," Cordelia noted, meaning Schuyler's forearms.

Schuyler nodded. Streaks of pale blue lines blossomed in an intricate pattern, visible under the skin's surface, on the underside of her forearms all the way to her wrist. The prominent blue veins had appeared a week shy of her fifteenth birthday. They didn't hurt, but they did itch. It was as if all of a sudden she was growing out of her skin—or *into* it—somehow.

"They look the same to me," Schuyler replied.

"Don't forget about your appointment with Dr. Pat."

Schuyler nodded.

Beauty made herself at home on Schuyler's duvet, looking out the window toward the river twinkling behind the trees.

Cordelia began to pat Beauty's smooth fur. "I had a dog like this once," she said. "When I was about your age. Your mother did, too." Cordelia smiled wistfully.

Her grandmother rarely talked about Schuyler's mother, who, technically, wasn't dead—she'd slipped into a coma when Schuyler was hardly a year old, and had been trapped in that state ever since. The doctors all agreed she registered normal brain activity, and that she could wake up at any moment. But she never had. Schuyler visited her mother every Sunday at the Columbia Presbyterian Hospital to read to her from the Sunday *Times*.

Schuyler didn't have many memories of her mother—apart from a sad, beautiful woman who sang lullabies to her in the crib. Maybe she just remembered that her mother looked sad because that's how she looked now, when she was asleep—there was a melancholy cast to her features. A lovely, sorrowful-looking woman with folded hands, her platinum hair fanned against the pillow.

She wanted to ask her grandmother more questions about her mother and her bloodhound—but the faraway look had left Cordelia's face, and Schuyler knew she wouldn't get any more tidbits about her mother that night.

"Dinner at six," her grandmother said, leaving the room.

"Yes, Cordelia," Schuyler mumbled.

She closed her eyes and lay on the bed, leaning against Beauty. The sun began to set through the blinds. Her grandmother was such an enigma. Schuyler wished, not for the first time, that she were a normal girl, with a normal family. She felt very lonely all of a sudden. She wondered if she should have told Oliver about Jack's note. She'd never kept something like that from him before. But she was worried he'd just call her silly for falling for some stupid joke.

Then her phone beeped. Oliver's number flashed on the text message, almost as if he knew how she was feeling right then.

MISS U BABE.

Schuyler smiled. She might not have parents. But at least she had one true friend.

ggie Carondolet's funeral had all the trappings of an exclusive society event. The Carondolets were a high-profile New York family, and Aggie's untimely death had been fodder for the tabloids. PREP SCHOOL GIRL DEAD IN DOWNTOWN CLUB. Her parents had shuddered, but there was nothing they could do about it. The city was obsessed with the beautiful, rich, and tragic. (The more beautiful, rich, and tragic, the bigger the headline.) That morning, a phalanx of photographers stood guard at the school's gates, waiting to get a shot of the grieving mother (a dignified Sloane Carondolet, 1985's deb of the year) and the stricken best friend, none other than lissome It-girl-about-town Mimi Force.

Once Mimi saw the photographers, she was glad she'd splurged on the Dior Homme suit by Hedi Slimane. It had been a bitch getting it tailored overnight, but what Mimi wanted, Mimi always got. The suit was of black satin, with sharp, severe lines. She wore nothing underneath but an onyx choker. She would look fabulous in tomorrow's papers—the soupçon of tragedy making her an even more glamorous figure.

Seating inside the Duchesne chapel was arranged according to rank, just like a fashion show. Of course, Mimi was given a front-row perch. She was seated between her father and her brother, the three of them making a good-looking trio. Her mother, stuck in a three-month plastic surgery safari in South Africa (facelifts disguised as vacations) couldn't return in time, so Gina Dupont, a beautiful art dealer and close friend of her father's, had accompanied him to the funeral.

Mimi knew Gina was actually one of her father's mistresses, but the knowledge didn't bother her. Growing up, she'd been shocked by the constancy of her parents' extra-marital affairs, but when she was old enough, she'd accepted the relationships for what they were—necessary to the *Caerimonia Osculor*. No one could be all things to one person. Marriage was for keeping the family fortune within the family, for making a good match, akin to a sound business deal. She'd been made to understand there were some things that could only be satisfied outside of a marriage, some things that even a loyal spouse couldn't provide.

She noticed Senator Llewellyn and his family entering through a side door. Bliss's stepmother strutted in wearing a floor-length black mink over a black dress; the senator was wearing a double-breasted black suit; Bliss was wearing a black cashmere sweater and slim black Gucci cigarette pants. Then Mimi noticed something odd. Bliss's little sister was dressed head to toe in white.

Who wears white to a funeral? But as Mimi looked around, she noticed almost half of the assembled guests in the chapel were wearing white—and all of them were sitting across the aisle. Sitting in the very front pew, leading the white-clad mourners was a small, wizened woman Mimi had never seen before. She noticed Oliver Hazard-Perry and his parents walk toward the front and bow to the white-garbed crone before finding seats in the far back.

The mayor and his entourage arrived, followed by the governor, his wife, and children. To the man, they were all in the appropriate black formal dress and sat themselves behind her father's pew. Mimi felt oddly relieved. Everyone on their side of the room was wearing the proper black or charcoal garments.

Mimi was glad for the closed coffin. She didn't want to see that frozen scream again, not in this lifetime. Anyway, it was all a big mistake. She was certain the Wardens would find some perfectly reasonable explanation for all this, some part of the cycle that explained the loss of all that blood. Because Aggie just couldn't be dead. As her father said, Aggie probably wasn't even in that coffin.

The service began, and the assembled rose from their seats and sang "Nearer, My God, to Thee." Mimi looked up from her hymnal and noticed Bliss leaving her seat. She raised an eyebrow. After the chaplain said the proper words, Aggie's sister made a brief eulogy. Several other students spoke, including her brother, Jack, who made a moving speech, and just as quickly, the service was over. Mimi followed her family as they left their pew.

The diminutive, white-haired matron who was sitting across from them walked over and tapped her father lightly on the arm. She had the bluest eyes Mimi had ever seen and was wearing an impeccable ivory Chanel suit and ropes of pearls around her wrinkled neck.

Charles Force startled visibly. Mimi had never seen her father that way. He was a composed, regal man, with a mane of silver hair and a rigid military bearing. The lines on his face were grooved with the consequences of power. It was said that Charles Force was the real authority that ran New York. The power behind the powerful.

"Cordelia," her father said to the old bat, with a bow of the head. "It is good to see you again."

"It has been too long." She had the clipped, nasal tones of a true Yankee.

He didn't respond. "A terrible loss," he said finally.

"Extremely unfortunate," the old lady agreed. "Although it could have been prevented."

"I'm not sure what you're talking about," Charles replied, looking genuinely perplexed.

"You know as well as I, that they should have been warned—"

"Enough. Not here," he said, lowering his voice and pulling her toward him. Mimi strained to hear the rest of the conversation.

"Always the first to shy from the truth. You are the way you have always been, arrogant and blind. . . ." the old woman was saying.

"And if we had listened to you and sown the fear? Where would we be then?" he asked coldly. "You would have us cowering in caves."

"I would have had us ensuring our survival. Instead, we are vulnerable once more," Cordelia replied, her raspy voice shaking with anger. "Instead, they are allowed to return, to hunt. If I had the authority, if the Conclave had listened to me, to Teddy—"

"But they did not, they chose me to lead, as I have always done," Charles interrupted smoothly. "But this is no time to bring up old wounds and grievances." He frowned. "Have you—no, you haven't—Mimi, Jack, come here."

"Ah, the twins." Cordelia smiled a cryptic smile. "Together again." Mimi didn't like the way the senile old thing was looking at her, sizing her up as if she knew everything about her already.

"This is Cordelia Van Alen," Charles Force said gruffly. "Cordelia, the twins. Benjamin and Madeleine."

"Pleased to make your acquaintance," Jack Force said politely.

"Ditto," Mimi snorted.

Cordelia nodded complacently. She turned to Charles Force once more and whispered fiercely. "You must raise the alarm! We must be vigilant! There is still time. We may still stop them, if you would only find it in your heart to forgive," she said. "Gabrielle . . ."

"Do not speak to me of Gabrielle," Charles said, cutting her off. "Never. I would never hear her name spoken to me again. Especially from you."

Who was Gabrielle? Mimi wondered. Why did her father seem so agitated? Mimi felt angry and annoyed to see how her father reacted to the old woman's words.

Cordelia's eyes softened. "It has been fifteen years," she said. "Is that not long enough?"

"It is good to see you well, Cordelia. Good day," Charles said, a finality to his tone.

The old hag frowned and walked away without another word. Mimi saw Schuyler Van Alen following her, looking back at them sheepishly, as if embarrassed by her grandmother's actions. As well she should be, Mimi thought.

"Dad, who was that?" Mimi asked, noticing her father looking spooked.

"Cordelia Van Alen," he replied heavily, then said no more. As if that explained everything.

"Who wears white to a funeral?" Mimi sneered, her lip curling.

"Black is the color of night," Charles muttered. "White is the true color of death." For a moment, he looked down at his black suit in dismay.

"Huh? Dad? What did you say?"

He shook his head, lost in thought.

Mimi noticed Jack run up to talk to Schuyler, and the two of them began an intense, whispered conversation. Mimi didn't like that one bit. She had no idea who this Schuyler person thought she was, and she didn't give a damn if it turned out she was Committee material after all. She didn't like the way Jack was looking at Schuyler. The only other person he ever looked at like that was her.

And Mimi wanted to keep it that way.

liss hadn't been able to stand it. While the service was still going on, she had decided she had to get out of there. Funerals freaked her out. The only one she'd ever been to was the one for her great-aunt, and no one had even been that sad. Bliss could have sworn she'd overheard her parents say "It's about time" and "Took her long enough" at the funeral. Great-Aunt Gertrude had lived to a ripe old age of 110 years—she'd been featured on the *Today* show—and when Bliss had visited her at the ranch the day before her death, the old thing was as spry as ever. "It's time for me to go, my dear. I know it is, but we shall meet again," she'd said to Bliss.

At least Aggie's wasn't an open casket, but it still made her feel queasy to think of a dead body in there, just a few feet away from her. Soon after they'd arrived, Bliss managed to wriggle out of sitting with her stepmother, who was too busy saying hello to all the other Duchesne moms anyway.

Bliss stealthily made her way toward the exit. She caught Mimi's eye on the way. Mimi raised an eyebrow and Bliss mouthed "bathroom," feeling a little silly for having to do so. Why did Mimi keep such close tabs on her? she wondered, as she continued her way toward the exit. Mimi was worse than her stepmother. It was getting irritating. She slunk out of the back door, only to run into someone else trying to sneak outside.

Dylan was wearing a narrow black suit, with a white shirt and a skinny black tie. He looked like a member of The Strokes. He smiled at her. "Going somewhere?"

"It's, uh, hot in there," she said lamely.

He nodded, pondering her statement. They hadn't really spoken to each other since Friday night, in the alley between the nightclubs. She'd been meaning to seek him out, just to apologize for ignoring him yesterday. Not that she had anything to apologize for, really. After all, they'd just spent the night talking. It wasn't like they were friends or anything. No big deal.

Except that it was. That night, he'd told her all about his family, and how he'd hated boarding school in Connecticut. She'd told him about Houston, how she used to drive her grandfather's Cadillac convertible to school, which everyone thought was hilarious. The thing was a boat—with proper fins. More important, she'd confessed how she didn't feel like she fit in at Duchesne at all, and how she didn't even like Mimi.

It was liberating to have been so honest with him, although she regretted it as soon as she got home, traumatized by the fear that somehow he would find a way to tell Mimi what she'd confided in him, even though she knew it was impossible. Mimi was in the In-Clique. Dylan hung out with the misfits and losers. Never the twain shall meet. If he even tried to approach Mimi, she would cut him dead with a look even before he got his mouth open.

"Wanna cut?" he asked. His black hair was combed straight back, and he wiggled his dark eyebrows at her invitingly.

Cutting a funeral. Now that was an interesting idea. The whole school was supposed to be at the service. It was mandatory. The only class Bliss had ever cut was gym, one afternoon when she and her friends decided to go see some teen slasher flick. It had been a fun day—the movie was even worse than it sounded, and they'd gotten back to school without getting caught.

At Duchesne, you were actually allowed to cut class twice a semester—it was part of the "flexible academic program." The school understood that sometimes, the stress was just too much and students occasionally had to cut class. It was amazing how even rebellion was written into the school's rules, everything so neatly tied into the whole rigor and logic of the place.

But as far as she knew, no one was allowed to cut a funeral. That would be seriously transgressive. Especially because she was supposed to be one of Aggie's BFF's since they hung out in the same crowd.

"Let's go," Dylan said, reaching out to hold her hand.

Bliss began to follow him, when another figure stepped out of the chapel doors. "Where are you going?" Jordan Llewellyn asked her sister, her large eyes boring into Bliss's skull.

"Who are you?" Dylan asked.

"Beat it, buttface," Bliss warned.

"You shouldn't go. It's not safe," Jordan said, looking directly at Dylan.

"Let's go, she's a freak," Bliss said, scowling at her sister, who was dressed all in white and looked like she was about to receive her first communion.

"I'm telling!" Jordan threatened.

"Go ahead! Tell everybody!" Bliss shot back.

Dylan smirked, and without another word, Bliss followed him through the back door, down the stairs, toward the first level of the mansion.

One of the school's housekeepers looked up from inside the copy room, which faced the back staircase. "Wha' you kids doing here?" she asked, putting a hand on her ample hips.

"Adriana, be cool." Dylan smiled.

The housekeeper shook her head, but she smiled back.

Bliss liked that Dylan was on friendly terms with the staff. Even though he was just being polite, it was still nice. Mimi treated the ground staff and the service workers with withering condescension.

Dylan led Bliss out the side door past the Dumpsters and out the service entrance. Soon they were free, and walking down Ninety-first Street.

"What do you want to do?" he asked.

She shrugged. She inhaled the fresh autumn air. Now, that was something she was really starting to enjoy about New York. The crisp, clean fall weather—they didn't have weather like that down in Houston. It went from muggy to rainy. She put her hands in the pockets of her calf-skimming Chloé trench coat.

"It's New York, we could do anything," he teased. "The whole city is open to us. We could see a burlesque show, or a bad comedy act. Hear some Derrida lecture at NYU. Or we could go bowling at the Piers. I know, what about this bar in the East Village where the waiters are real Belgian monks? Or maybe we could go rowing in the Park?"

"Maybe we can just walk to a museum?" she asked.

"Oh, artsy girl." He smiled. "All right. Which one?"

"The Met," she decided. She'd only been there once, and only to the gift shop, where her stepmother had spent hours picking out floral prints for souvenirs.

They walked toward Fifth Avenue and arrived at the Metropolitan Museum in quick time. The front steps were filled with people scarfing down their lunches, taking pictures, or simply basking in the sun. It was a carnival atmosphere; someone was slapping bongos on one end, and a boom box blasted reggae music on the other. They walked up the steps and inside.

The lobby of the museum was bustling with activity and color—schoolchildren on field trips lined up behind their teachers, art students walked briskly with their sketchbooks tucked underneath their arms, a Babelian prattle of many different languages bubbled from the tourists.

Dylan slid a dime underneath the glass ticket counter. "Two, please," he said, an innocent smile on his face.

Bliss was a little appalled. She checked the sign. SUGGESTED DONATION: $15. Well, he had a point, it was suggested, not mandatory. The cashier handed them their round Met pins with no comment. Apparently, he'd seen it all before.

"Have you ever been to the Temple of Dendur?" Dylan asked, leading Bliss toward the northern end of the museum.

"No," she said, shaking her head. "What's that?"

"Stop," he said. He put his hands gently on her face. "Close your eyes."

"Why?" She giggled.

"Just do it," he said. "Trust me."

She closed her eyes, holding a hand against her face, and she felt him tug at her hand, leading her forward. She walked hesitantly, feeling ahead of her—they were inside some kind of maze, she thought—as he led her briskly through a series of sharp turns. Then they were outside of it. Even with her eyes closed, she could sense they were in a large, empty space.

"Open your eyes," Dylan whispered.

She blinked them open.

They were standing in front of the ruins of an Egyptian temple. The building was majestic and primitive at the same time—in direct contrast to the clean, modern lines of the museum. It was absolutely stunning. The hall was empty, and there was a long horizontal fountain in front of the temple. It was a breathtaking piece of art, and the history behind it—the fact that the museum had meticulously shipped and reconstructed it so that the temple looked perfectly at home in a Manhattan museum—made Bliss's head roll.

"Oh my God."

"I know," Dylan said, his eyes twinkling.

Bliss blinked back tears. It was the most romantic thing anyone had ever done to her—ever.

He looked directly into her eyes, nodding his head down toward her lips.

She fluttered her eyelashes, her heart racing in her chest, swooning. She leaned toward him, lifting her face to be kissed. He looked gentle and hopeful, and there was something appealingly vulnerable about the way he couldn't meet her gaze.

Their lips met.

And that's when it happened.

The world went gray. She was in her skin but not in her skin. The room was constricting. The world was shrinking. All four walls of the temple were suddenly whole. She was in the desert. She could taste the acrid sand in her mouth, feel the hot sun on her back. A thousand scarabs—black and shiny, buzzing—flew out of the temple door. And that was when she began to scream.

Catherine Carver's Diary
30th of November, 1620
Plymouth, Massachusetts

Today Myles Standish took a team down the coast
to Roanoke, to bring medicine, food and supplies
to the settlement there. It is a fortnight's sail, so
they will be gone a good while. I was heartsick to
see John go off with the men. So far, we have been
safe, but who knows for how long. No one dares say.
The children grow quickly and are a delight to
all. There has been an abundance of twin births.
The Allertons recently had triplets. Susannah
White, whose husband, William, also journeyed
to Roanoke, came to visit. We agreed it is a fertile
season. We have been blessed.

-C.C.

ELEVEN

Schuyler was still thinking about what Jack had said after Aggie's funeral when she arrived at Dr. Pat's all-white office in a chrome-and-glass Fifth Avenue tower later that afternoon. He'd asked her why she had ignored his note, and she'd explained she had simply dismissed it as a prank. "You think Aggie's death is funny?" he'd asked, his face stricken. She had tried to protest—but her grandmother was calling her and she had to leave. She couldn't erase the look on his face. As if she had disappointed him deeply somehow. She blew out her bangs loudly. Why did he have such an effect on her? An emaciated woman in a fox-fur jacket across the room glared at her. Schuyler stared defiantly back.

Cordelia had made a big to-do about Schuyler seeing Dr. Pat. The doctor was some kind of dermatologist, a famous one. The office was more like the inside of a Miami hotel—the Shore Club or the Delano—than a normal waiting room. It was all white, white flokati rugs, white tile walls, white lacquer tables, white leather couches, white fiberglass Eames loungers. Apparently Dr. Pat was *the* Dr. Pat, the one who all the socialites and fashion designers and celebrities credited with their fabulous complexions. Several signed and framed photographs from models and actresses hung on the walls.

Schuyler pushed Jack out of her mind and began flipping through the glossy magazine articles extolling the doctor's virtues, when the door from the inner office opened and Mimi Force walked out.

"What are *you* doing here?" Mimi spat. She had changed out of her Dior suit and was wearing a more "casual" outfit—a pair of tight four-thousand-dollar Apo jeans with the platinum rivets and a diamond button, a chunky Martine Sitbon sweater, and slim butter-colored Jimmy Choo stilettos.

"Sitting down?" Schuyler replied, even though it was obvious Mimi had asked a rhetorical question. "What happened to your face?"

Mimi glared. Her whole face was covered with little pinpoints of blood. She'd just received a laser dermabrasion peel, and it had left her skin a little raw. It helped mask the blue veins that were starting to fade around her eyes. "None of your business."

Schuyler shrugged.

Mimi left, slamming the door behind her.

A few minutes later, the nurse called Schuyler's name, and she was ushered into a treatment room. The nurse took her weight and blood pressure, then asked her to change into a backless hospital gown. Schuyler put on the gown and waited a few minutes before the doctor finally entered.

Dr. Pat was a stern, gray-haired woman, who looked at Schuyler and said, "You're very thin," as a greeting.

Schuyler nodded. It never mattered what she ate—she could live on chocolate cakes and French fries and she never seemed to gain an ounce. She'd been that way since she was a kid. Oliver always used to marvel at her capacity. "You should be as big as a house," he liked to say, "the way you eat."

Dr. Pat inspected the marks on her arms, silently tracing the patterns that had formed there. "Do you get dizzy?"

Schuyler nodded. "Sometimes."

"Like you can't remember where you are or where you've been?"

"Uh-huh."

"Do you ever feel like you're dreaming but you're not?"

Schuyler frowned. "I'm not sure what you mean."

"How old are you?"

"Fifteen."

"Right on time then," Dr. Pat muttered. "But no flash-back memories yet. Hmm."

"Excuse me?"

She suddenly remembered that night at The Bank.

Oliver had gone to get drinks, and she'd excused herself to go to the ladies' room. But when she'd turned the corner, she'd bumped into that strange man. She had only seen him for a moment—a tall man, with broad shoulders wearing a dark suit—his bright gray eyes had glared at her from the darkness. Then he had disappeared, although there was only a blank wall where he had been standing. There had been something ancient and remote about him, and she couldn't place it, but he seemed familiar. She didn't know if that was anything to tell Dr. Pat about, so she didn't mention it.

The doctor took out a prescription pad and began scribbling on it. "I'm going to give you some cream to cover your veins for now, but really, it's nothing to worry about. I'll see you in the spring."

"Why? Is something going to happen in the spring?"

But the doctor wouldn't say.

Schuyler left the doctor's office with more questions than she had answers.

Whenever Mimi felt upset, she went shopping. It was her natural reaction to any intense emotional experience. Happy or sad, depressed or triumphant, she could only be found in one place. She stormed out of the doctor's office, took the carpeted elevator to the ground floor, and walked across Madison to the haven of Barneys. Mimi loved Barneys. Barneys was to Mimi as Tiffany's was to Holly Golightly, a place where nothing terrible could ever be allowed to happen. She loved the clean lines of the beauty counters, the pale wood fixtures, the glass cases displaying tiny, exquisite and exorbitantly priced jewelry, the small selection of Italian handbags, everything so clean and modern and perfect.

It was a great antidote to everything that had happened—because of course, Aggie was still dead. That's what scared her the most. Her death meant there was something The Committee was keeping from them. That there was something they didn't know, or something The Wardens weren't telling them. She didn't want to question them, but it was maddening when her father wasn't forthcoming with any answers.

And that Van Alen girl—the one with the spooky grandmother—showing up at Dr. Pat's office like that. There was something about that girl she didn't like, and not just because Jack seemed to be interested in her. A wave of revulsion had washed over her when she saw the two of them together, and she wanted to exorcise the remaining ill feeling that had made her feel like vomiting. She wished her brother would quit hanging around scraggly sophomores like Schuyler Van Alen. What was wrong with him?

A woman in a sleek pantsuit approached Mimi deferentially. "Would you like to see anything I've put aside for you, Miss Force?"

Mimi nodded. She followed her personal shopper to the private dressing room in the back that was reserved for VIPs and celebrities. It was a circular room, with suede couches, a small bar, and a hosted buffet table. In the middle of the room was a rack of clothes that her shopper had selected especially for her.

She took a chocolate-dipped strawberry from a silver tray and chewed on it slowly while she perused the racks. She'd already made her fall purchases that August, but it didn't hurt to see if she'd missed any trends. She caressed a gold Lanvin ball gown, a shorn Prada jacket, and a floral Derek Lam cocktail dress.

"I'll take these," Mimi said. "And what do we have here?" she cooed, finding a wisp of chiffon on a padded hanger.

She brought the dress into the dressing room and emerged a few minutes later in a devastating leopard print Roberto Cavalli silk gown. She looked at herself in the mirror. The dress was slashed down from neck to navel, revealing her pale, ivory skin, and ended in a haze of feathers that fluttered down her calves.

"Bellissima."

Mimi looked up. A handsome Italian man was staring at her, his eyes resting on her exposed cleavage.

She covered herself with her hands and displayed her curvy back to him. Her black thong peeked above the waist. "Zip me up?"

He walked over and put a finger underneath the strap of her thong, toying with the lacy fabric. Her skin tingled with goose bumps at his touch. He stroked the crescent underside of her back, stopping right above her lower hip. He smiled at her in the mirror and she returned his smolder. He looked to be in his early twenties, twenty-three tops. A gold Patek Philippe glinted on his wrist. She recognized him from the society pages. A famous Manhattan playboy, who was rumored to have sent half the society girls in the 10021 ZIP code into therapy.

"That dress is wasted on you here," he said, as he pulled the zipper up slowly.

Mimi took a step back, arching her neck and observing how the dress barely covered her nipples. Definite side cleavage.

"Then why don't we go somewhere else?" Mimi asked, her eyes sparkling dangerously. She could sense the blood beneath his skin, almost taste the rich, luscious, pulp in his veins. No wonder she'd been feeling irritable and weak—with all the distress from Aggie's funeral, she'd hardly had any time for a new boy.

Some people would probably advise a young girl not to step inside a stranger's Lamborghini. But as Mimi folded her legs inside the passenger seat, her black Barneys shopping bags safely stowed in the trunk, she could only smile to herself. She was still wearing the Roberto Cavalli dress.

He revved up the engine and powered the accelerator, quickly shifting gears so that the flat, yellow sportscar screeched up Madison. He gazed at her with a predatory hunger, and when he placed his right arm over her backrest, he rested a heavy hand on her shoulder.

Instead of protesting, Mimi drew his hand farther down so that it rested on her cleavage, feeling exhilarated as he squeezed her breast through the thin fabric with the one hand, and with the other, maneuvered the car deftly down the avenue.

"Is good, yes?" he asked with a heavy Italian accent.

"Very good." She licked her lips slowly.

He had no idea what he was in for.

TWELVE

"Tell me again what happened."

Bliss sat on the white leather recliner in Dr. Pat's office. Her parents had made the appointment after she'd woken them up last night, screaming her lungs out.

"Yesterday, you were at the temple," Dr. Pat prodded.

"Right. The Egyptian wing at the Met," Bliss agreed. "He'd just taken his hands away from my eyes, and I saw the temple." She was sitting on a white Eames fiberglass lounge chair in a treatment room. She wasn't exactly sure what kind of doctor "Dr. Pat" was. It looked like a dermatologist's office, but she also saw several pregnant women getting ultrasounds in the other rooms.

"Yes, you said that."

"And then—" She blushed. "I think he was about to kiss me. I think he did kiss me, but then, I don't know—I blacked out. The next thing I knew, I was just walking around with him in the American wing looking at furniture."

"And that's all you remember?"

"I remember screaming."

"You were screaming?"

"No, someone was screaming. Far away." Bliss said. She looked around at Dr. Pat's office. It was the cleanest, whitest office she had ever been in. She noticed that even the medical instruments gleamed and were arranged artfully in Italian glass canisters.

"Tell me about it."

Bliss reddened. She hadn't decided to reveal what bothered her so much. Her parents already thought she was crazy—what if Dr. Pat did too?

"Well, it was really weird, but all of a sudden, I was standing outside the temple, when it was still whole. In Egypt, I mean. The sun was really bright, and the temple—it wasn't a ruin. It was complete. And I was there. It was like, being inside a movie."

Suddenly Dr. Pat smiled. It was so unexpected, Bliss found herself grinning back. "I know that sounds insane, but I felt like I was transported back in time."

Now Dr. Pat was definitely cheerful. She folded up her notebook and put it away. "What you're experiencing is perfectly normal."

"It is?" Bliss asked.

"Regenerative Memory Syndrome."

"What is that?"

Dr. Pat provided a long-winded explanation about the effects of "cell restructuring cognizance phenomenon," a cataclysmic event in the brain that produced the subsequent "time-warp" effect. Her explanation went completely over Bliss's head. "It's like déjà vu. It happens to the best of us."

"I guess. So I'm not crazy? Other people have experienced this?"

"Well, not everybody," Dr. Pat replied doubtfully. "But some people. Special people. You should have told your parents about it sooner. You have a Committee meeting on Monday, yes?"

How did Dr. Pat know about The Committee?

She nodded.

"Everything will be explained in time. For now, don't give it another thought."

"So there's nothing wrong with me?"

"Absolutely nothing at all."

Later that night, Bliss woke up with a blistering headache. Where am I? she wondered. She felt as though she'd been hit by a truck. Her body felt waterlogged and heavy, and her head was groggy. She looked at the clock next to her bed.

It flashed 11:49 P.M.

With effort, she pulled herself up to a sitting position. She put a hand to her forehead. She was hot, burning. The pounding in her head was merciless. Her stomach growled. *Hungry*.

She swung her feet over her bed and heaved herself up to stand. Not a good idea. She was dizzy and sick. She grabbed on to one of the bedposts and staggered over to the light switch. When she reached over to turn on the light, her bedroom was suddenly illuminated.

Everything was just as she'd left it—the thick Committee letter and forms scattered on her desk, her German textbook open to the same page, her fountain pens arranged neatly in her pencil box, a funny Stetson magnet from her friends back home in Texas, a framed photograph of her family in front of the Capitol steps when her father was sworn in to the Senate.

She wiped her eyes and patted down her curls, which, from experience, she knew were sticking out frantically in all directions.

Hungry.

It was a dark, abiding ache. A physical pain. This was new. Dr. Pat didn't say anything about *this*. She clutched her stomach, feeling nauseous. She walked outside her bedroom to the darkened hallway, following the low lights to the kitchen.

Their stainless-steel kitchen looked severe in the midnight glow of the overhead lamps. Bliss saw her reflection on all the surfaces—a tall, gangly girl with scary hair and a bleak expression.

She opened the door to the Sub-Zero. Arranged neatly in rows were bottles of Vitamin Water, Pellegrino, and Veuve

Clicquot. She tore open the drawers. Fresh fruit, cut and placed in Tupperware containers. Creamline Yogurt. A half-eaten grapefruit covered in cellophane. White cardboard containers of leftover Chinese food.

No good.

Hunnngrrry.

In the meat drawer, she found it. A pound of raw hamburger meat. She took it out and tore the brown paper wrapping. Meat. She stuffed her face with the bloody chunks of ground beef, devouring it voraciously, so that the blood dripped down her chin.

She practically swallowed it whole.

"What are you doing?"

Bliss froze.

Her sister, Jordan, in pink flannel pajamas, was standing in the doorway of the kitchen, watching her.

"It's all right, Jordan." BobiAnne suddenly appeared out of the shadows. She was smoking a cigarette in the corner. When she exhaled, the smoke curled up around the edges of her lips. "Go to bed."

Bliss put the packet of meat down on the counter. She wiped her lips with a napkin. "I don't know what got into me. I was just hungry."

"Of course you are, my dear," BobiAnne agreed, as if it were the most normal thing in the world to find your stepdaughter eating a hunk of raw hamburger meat straight from the fridge at three in the morning. "There are some filet mignons in the second drawer. In case you still have an appetite."

And with those words, BobiAnne bade her goodnight.

Bliss thought about it for a moment, wondering if the world had gone insane. Dr. Pat telling her her out-of-body, out-of-time experience was just "one of those things," her stepmother not blinking an eye at seeing her covered in blood in the kitchen. She contemplated for a moment. Then she found the packet of steaks and ate them, too.

Consumption. Symptoms include a high fever, fainting, dizziness, coughing up of blood, and the accumulation of fluid in the lungs. During the early years of the American colony at Plymouth, a high degree of consumption was the cause of many deaths. "Full consumption" was the term for a person who had died with all of his or her blood drained from the body. Theories suggest that a bacterial infection broke down the platelets, thinning out the blood and absorbing it into the body so that it only looked as though all the blood had disappeared.

—From *Death and Life in the Plymouth Colonies, 1620–1641*
by Professor Lawrence Winslow Van Alen

THIRTEEN

*T*he next day, the whole upper school was called into the chapel again, but for a less somber reason. It was a Career Talk. Even the unfortunate demise of one of their students couldn't change the rigid schedule of lectures that the school had planned for the year. Part of the Duchesne philosophy was to expose their students to a sampling of the many career opportunities and paths available to them. They'd had talks from a famous heart surgeon, the editor of a prestigious magazine, the CEO of a Fortune 500 company, a famous film director. Most of the adults who came to give the talks were Duchesne alumni, or Duchesne parents. Most of the students welcomed the hour-and-a-half break in their day, since it meant that they could snooze in the back pews, which was a lot more comfortable than nodding off in class.

"We have a special treat for you today," the Dean of

Students announced. "Today we have Linda Farnsworth, from Farnsworth Models." A ripple of approval and excitement went through the assemblage.

Farnsworth Models was the biggest name in the cutthroat modeling industry. Their biannual Career Talk at Duchesne was just an excuse to find the newest batch of models lurking in the student body. An incongruous, but unimpeachable fact was that Duchesne was a breeding ground for modeling talent in the city. Students had gyrated their hips in music videos, walked the runways in Bryant Park, and had appeared in television commercials and print advertising. An inordinate number were featured in the J. Crew and Abercrombie & Fitch catalogs. The Duchesne type—tall, willowy, blond, aristocratic, and all-American, was more in demand than ever.

Linda Farnsworth was a short, squat woman with crinkly hair and a dowdy appearance. She wore half-moon glasses, and her voice quavered over the microphone as she explained the ins and outs of the modeling industry. She exhorted its virtues (Glamorous photo shoots! Travel to exotic places! Fun parties!), and in the same breath emphasized the very hard work that went into making the perfect photographs. There was a smattering of polite applause when she finished.

When the formal talk ended, Linda set up a casting call on the third-floor landing and invited any interested students to try out. Almost all of the girls and even a few of the boys waited in line to see if they would make the cut.

After a bunch of glum freshmen were ushered to the side, Mimi stepped forward. She had dressed especially well for the occasion, in a slim-fitting tailored C&C California T-shirt and low, hip-slung Paige jeans. She'd heard that models should dress as plainly as possible for auditions, a blank canvas on which advertisers and designers could easier project their visions. The night before, she'd left the Italian exhausted in his penthouse loft, she herself felt invigorated and cheerful.

"Walk up toward the end of the staircase and back, please," Linda instructed.

Linda clucked in approval as Mimi stomped up and down the hallway and pirouetted at the end of the stairs.

"You have the ideal proportions my dear, and a natural ability. A fabulous walk is what it's all about, you know. Tell me, are you interested in being a model?"

"Of course!" Mimi squealed, clapping her hands together, delighted she had been chosen. It was about time she joined the ranks of the professionally beautiful!

Bliss was next. She galloped up and down the hallway, swinging her arms. She still felt queasy thinking about the pound of hamburger she'd wolfed down the night before, even though eating it had made her feel better. She still thought it was strange that BobiAnne had seemed to take the whole incident in stride.

"Walk's a little rough, darling, but very teachable. Yes, we must have you at Farnsworth," Linda decided.

Mimi and Bliss hugged each other in joy. Bliss saw Dylan watching them from the corner of the great hall. She smiled tentatively at him. He saluted her in return. She hoped he hadn't noticed anything unusual about her when they were in the Met. Dr. Pat had explained that during Regenerative Memory Syndrome, part of her was in the present, but the part that was conscious had been in the past. The memory blackouts wouldn't last that long—maybe four, five minutes tops. It bothered her that the part that would remember whether they'd kissed or not had been absent for that crucial juncture. She didn't even know how to act around him—were they dating or what? Just friends? It was maddening not to know where she stood with a boy she liked. Okay, so there it was. She liked him. She liked him so much she was even starting to not care about what Mimi would think of the two of them getting together.

Bliss looked at Mimi a tad resentfully. Even if she owed her social life and current status to Mimi, she balked at having to answer to her for everything.

The bell for the next class rang, and a harried girl rushed past the modeling station without even glancing at the gathering. Schuyler had slept through the entire lecture, since she'd hardly gotten any sleep the night before.

Linda Farnsworth stopped her in her tracks breaking her reverie. "Hello! And who might you be?"

"Schuyler Van Alen?" Schuyler replied. Why did she do

that? Why couldn't she be more confident? "I mean, I'm Schuyler," she said, frantically brushing her bangs away from her eyes.

"Are you interested in modeling?"

"Her—a model?" Mimi spat from the sidelines where she was filling out the Farnsworth client contract. She eyed Schuyler balefully.

"Shhh," Bliss said, embarrassed enough to elbow Mimi for once.

Schuyler overheard them. She looked down at what she was wearing—torn black stockings with ladders in both knees (already rating her a dress code demerit), a loose-fitting floral granny-dress with a drop waist, chunky gray socks because she couldn't find her black ones, her duct-taped sneakers, and a pair of half-moon glasses. Plus, she hadn't washed her hair in weeks. It's not like she would even want to be a model, so Mimi had nothing to worry about. A secret part of her was desperately flattered, although she tried not to be overly vain about her looks.

"No, I don't think so," Schuyler replied, smiling apologetically.

"But you have the look of a young Kate Moss!" Linda Farnsworth argued. "Can I take a Polaroid?"

Linda took a photo with her camera before Schuyler could protest.

Schuyler shielded her eyes. "Okay . . ."

"Write your number down here. You don't need to sign,

but if we find a designer who wants to use you, I'll call you, is that all right?"

"I guess." She agreed, scribbling her number down without a second thought. "Look, I really have to go."

Mimi glared at Schuyler and stalked off, her nose in the air. Bliss hung back and caught Schuyler's eye. "Congrats, by the way," Bliss said quietly. "I got picked, too."

"Uh, yeah, thanks, I guess," Schuyler said, shocked that anyone who hung around Mimi Force would even talk to her.

"Are you headed to art?" Bliss asked in a friendly way.

"Er . . ." Schuyler hesitated, not sure what the Texan girl wanted. To her relief, she noticed Oliver by the water fountain and turned away from Bliss without giving her a second thought.

"Hey there," she said.

"Oh, hey, Sky." He greeted her, looping an arm around her thin shoulders. They walked up the back stairs hidden in the administration corridor to the garret room for art class. Dylan was already there and grinning at them from behind his potters' wheel. He had an apron around his waist and his hands were covered in mud up to his elbows.

"Don't you just love getting dirty?" he asked.

They snickered approvingly and took a seat on each side of him. Schuyler set up her easel and Oliver took out his woodcuts. Neither of them noticed Bliss Llewellyn across the room, watching the three of them intensely.

In between brushstrokes, Schuyler happened to look up

and saw Jack Force leaning over Kitty Mullins's table, admiring her sculpture of a Siamese cat. She noticed a telltale hickey on Kitty's neck.

She wasn't the only one who saw them. Oliver raised his eyebrows but made no comment, and she was glad. She guessed Jack had found a girlfriend. Schuyler wondered if he was passing *her* oblique notes in class. Huh. That sure hadn't taken him long. She felt a wave of irritation prickling at her consciousness, but she brushed it away.

Oliver mimed hacking at Jack's back with an invisible axe. She smothered a laugh and put Jack Force out of her mind once and for all.

liss looked up from her canvas. Their art teacher was gesturing effusively over her landscape, but she wasn't listening. Her gaze kept drifting across the room, to where Dylan was sitting.

He hadn't even made any indication that he noticed her. Sure, he was perfectly friendly whenever they bumped into each other. And that was the problem—he was simply friendly. Maybe they hadn't even kissed at the Met that afternoon after all. Maybe nothing had happened. Maybe he'd lost interest, which was a blow to her ego as well as her psyche.

It was just so unfair, especially since she was now totally obsessed with him. She was starting to think about him way too much for just a casual friend-who-wasn't-even-in-her-clique. The actor had called, the model had begged for a date, but all she could think about was the way Dylan's dark sideburns curled around his ears, and the way he'd looked at her with his big, sad eyes. She could tell he was the kind of boy who broke the rules and let anything happen, and she liked that about him. It excited her.

She watched him interact with his friends—that goth girl who'd just been chosen as a model, and that cute, skinny guy with the shaggy hair—and felt a pang of jealousy. Dylan was clowning around, throwing mud at them, but they didn't seem to mind. The three of them seemed to be having a lot of fun.

When class was over, there was a bottleneck at the door—since the stairway was so narrow, everyone had to go single file. Bliss found herself standing right next to Dylan. She smiled at him tentatively. "Hey."

"*Après vous*, madame," he said gallantly, offering her the way.

She nodded her thanks, lingering to see if he would say anything else—maybe even ask her out again. But he didn't say a word. She walked down the stairs alone while he waited for his friends. She felt defeated.

After lunch with Mimi and her crew, Bliss walked down to the basement to grab books for her next class. She found Schuyler changing into her gym clothes in the hallway, standing right in front of her locker, while a bunch of other kids did the same, girls and boys alike in various stages of undress.

The school was an odd mix of luxury and penury—on the one hand, there was a state-of-the-art theater in the basement, complete with auditorium seating for two hundred, but there were no locker rooms because they didn't fit in the mansion. Students were encouraged to change in the bathrooms, but since they only had five minutes to do so, most ignored the rules and changed in the hallway to save time. The girls had perfected a removing-the-bra-through-the-side-armhole-and-putting-on-a-sports-bra-while-hiding-underneath-a-huge-T-shirt maneuver. The boys didn't even bat an eyelash.

One of the quirky things about Duchesne was that since they had all known each other since kindergarten, a sibling-like camaraderie prevailed. The teenage striptease only bothered the faculty, especially the errant history professor who happened to chance upon a half-naked junior in the hallway, eliciting malicious giggles—but there was nothing they could do to stop it. Dressing in public was just one of those odd things that was part of the Duchesne experience.

"Hey, can I talk to you for a bit?" Bliss asked, leaning against a locker and watching as Schuyler disappeared underneath an oversized sweatshirt. Being new, Bliss was one of the few girls who used the restroom to change. She couldn't quite feel as comfortable as everyone else did. Mimi, for instance, liked to parade in her La Petite Coquette bras as if she were walking on the beach in St. Tropez.

"Mfff?" Schuyler asked, a bump underneath the fabric,

her elbows pointing sideways and upward in an attempt to shove herself into her gym outfit. She took off the sweatshirt with a flourish and emerged in an oversized T-shirt and baggy sweat pants.

"What's on your mind?" she asked Bliss, regarding her a little warily.

"You're friends with Dylan Ward, aren't you?"

Schuyler shrugged. "Yeah. What about him?" She checked her watch. The second bell was going to ring soon, and kids from her class were already hurrying up the stairs to the lower court gyms.

"I just—do you know him well?"

Schuyler shrugged again. She wasn't sure what Bliss was asking. Of course she knew him well. She and Oliver were his only friends.

"I've heard rumors," Bliss said, looking around to see if anyone was listening to their conversation.

"Oh yeah, what?" Schuyler raised an eyebrow. She stuffed her sweatshirt in her locker.

"Well, that he was involved in some accident with some girl in Connecticut this summer—"

"I haven't heard anything about that," Schuyler said, cutting her off. "But people around here talk about everybody. Do you really believe that story?"

Bliss looked shocked. "Not at all! I don't believe it one bit."

"Look, I should go," Schuyler said brusquely, shouldering her tennis racket and walking away.

"Hold on," Bliss called, walking next to Schuyler and hurrying to keep up as Schuyler loped up the stairs.

"What?"

"I just . . . I mean . . ." Bliss shrugged. "I'm sorry we got off on the wrong foot. My bad, okay? Can we start over? Please?"

Schuyler narrowed her eyes. The second bell rang. "I'm late," she said flatly.

"It's just, we went to the Met the other day and I thought we had a really nice time, but I don't know, he hasn't spoken to me since," Bliss explained. "Do you know if he has a girl-friend or anything?"

Schuyler sighed. If she was late for class her grandmother would get a note. Duchesne didn't have anything like "deten-tion"; the only punishments it meted out were tattletale notes home to overly involved parents who would commit hara-kiri if their kids didn't get into Harvard. She looked at Bliss, tak-ing in her nervous demeanor and hopeful smile.

Reluctantly, Schuyler came to the conclusion that maybe Bliss wasn't one of those Mimi clones after all. She didn't have pin-straight blond hair or sport an obnoxious "Team Force" insignia on her gym hoodie like the rest of Mimi's gang, for one. "As far as I know, he isn't dating anybody. He did mention meeting someone the other night at a club. . . ." Schuyler allowed finally, watching Bliss's reaction.

Bliss blushed.

"I thought so." Schuyler nodded. Against her better

judgment, she found herself relenting. If Dylan had taken her to the Met, Bliss really couldn't be all bad. Schuyler wasn't sure Mimi would even know what the Met was. Mimi's life revolved around shopping and getting into VIP rooms. She probably thought "the Met" was some kind of nightclub.

"If you want my advice, take it easy on him. I think he really likes you," she said, giving Bliss a sympathetic smirk.

"He does? I mean, he's talked about me?"

Schuyler rolled her shoulders. "It's really none of my business," she said, hesitating.

"What?"

"Well, I doubt he'd mind if you asked him to the fall dance. He probably would never even think of going himself, but he might go if you asked."

Bliss smiled. The dance was tomorrow night. She could do that. Her parents would have to let her go—it was a school event, and there were bound to be tons of chaperones there to appease their anxiety. "Thanks."

"No problem," Schuyler said, running up the stairs without giving Bliss a backward glance.

Struck by the idea, Bliss scribbled a quick note and tore off the paper from her binder. She carefully removed all the broken bits on the side, spritzed it with her perfume, and stuffed it in Dylan's locker.

She was shocked at her brazenness. She had never needed to pursue a boy before. But there's always a first time for everything.

FIFTEEN

*T*he yearly Duchesne back-to-school dance was called the Fall "Informals," although it was anything but informal. The dance was held at the historical headquarters of the American Society, a grand red brick mansion on Park Avenue and Sixty-eighth Street. The society was an organization dedicated to keeping an archive of early American history, including documents from the first colonies and the *Mayflower* journey. The second floor housed a wood-paneled library with a barrel-vaulted ceiling as well as several cozy, clubby rooms ideal for dinner and dancing. It was a popular event space, and many brides-to-be shelled out a fortune for the privilege of having their wedding on Park Avenue. But for Duchesne students, it was just the place where they had their school dance.

Earlier that evening, Oliver and Schuyler were hanging out in his room, doing nothing as usual—but when Schuyler casually mentioned she'd heard that Dylan—of all people—was going to the lame dance, Oliver pounced on the idea.

"Let's go."

"Us? Why?" Schuyler was horrified.

"C'mon, it'll be funny."

"No it won't." Schuyler argued. "Us go to some snobby dance? Just to see Mimi Force lording it over everyone?"

"I heard they do a pretty good spread," Oliver wheedled.

"I'm not hungry."

"C'mon, what else are we going to do?"

After the excitement of the past weekend, when they'd ventured to The Bank, it did seem a bit dull to just sit on Oliver's bed reading magazines together.

"All right," Schuyler agreed. "But I need to go home and change."

"Of course."

When Oliver picked her up, Schuyler was wearing a cocktail-length fifties-style black lace prom dress, dainty white wrist gloves, fishnet stockings, and round-toe high heels, almost as a joke. She'd found the dress on eBay for thirty dollars. The strapless dress fit perfectly around her tiny waist, and the skirt blossomed out at the hips like a graceful bell held aloft by a layer of tulle petticoats. She'd found her grandmother's pearl necklace, with the black satin ribbon, in the bottom of her music box, and tied it around her neck. Oliver had chosen a deep blue silk smoking jacket over a black shirt and black wool pants. He presented Schuyler with a breathtaking rose corsage.

"Where did you get it?" Schuyler asked as he slipped it around her wrist.

"You can have anything delivered in New York." Oliver grinned. He handed her a boutonniere, and she pinned it on his lapel.

"How do we look?"

"Perfect," he said, offering her his arm.

When they arrived at the American Society mansion, a host of sleek black town cars were dropping off students paired off in dates. The girls were in chic black cocktail dresses and pearls, the guys in blue blazers and wool trousers. No one had corsages. Instead, the girls were carrying long-stemmed calla lilies, which they carelessly tossed aside when they entered the room.

"I guess we didn't get the memo," Schuyler quipped.

They headed upstairs, trying to blend in. Several girls whispered when they saw Schuyler in her dress. "It's got to be from Marc Jacobs," someone whispered. "More like a costume shop," her friend sniffed. Schuyler turned crimson from embarrassment.

They found Dylan on the second landing by the cornucopia display. He was wearing a camel-hair sportscoat over a sharp black dress shirt and well-cut wool trousers. Bliss Llewellyn, the pretty redhead from Texas, was sitting on his lap. She was wearing a slim Costume National black sheath dress, Prada slingbacks, and the ubiquitous string of pearls around her swanlike neck.

"Hey guys," Dylan said, when he saw his friends. He shook hands with Oliver and pecked Schuyler on the cheek. "Y'all know Bliss, right?"

They nodded. Since when did Dylan say "Y'all"? He must really be into this girl.

"You clean up nice," Schuyler teased, brushing a piece of lint off Dylan's jacket.

"Is that Hugo Boss?" Oliver mocked, pretending to inspect the material.

"Yes, and don't get it dirty," Dylan shot back, chagrined but grinning nonetheless.

Bliss smiled happily at them. She winked at Schuyler. "Cool dress," she said, and it sounded like she actually meant it.

"Thanks."

"So—have you checked out the place? Some good eats upstairs," Dylan said.

"No—but we will," Oliver promised. They left the couple and wormed their way through the crowd upstairs to the buffet.

The rooms had been decorated with white Christmas lights, and in the back, there was an elegant display of hot and cold roast meats, silver plates laden with exquisite hors d'oeuvres and French pastries. In the middle room, a sweaty mix of patrician girls and rich boys were gyrating to the beat of a hard rap song. The lights were off, and Schuyler could only make out the shadows of their faces. She could see that all the boys from Duchesne were carrying little silver Tiffany hip flasks that stuck out of their side pants pockets. Occasionally, they would surreptitiously take a swig or pour a bit of alcohol in their date's cups. Even Oliver had brought his monogrammed one. There were several teachers milling about, but no one seemed to notice, or care about the covert tippling.

"Want a sip?"

"Sure," Schuyler said, taking the flask from his hand. The liquor was warm and hit the back of her throat. Her head buzzed for a minute, and she took a couple more gulps.

"Easy there! That's 181 proof," Oliver warned. "You're going to get wasted," he said gleefully.

But Schuyler felt just as sober as before, although she smiled and pretended to feel its effects.

They stood tentatively at the edge of the party, nursing their silver cups of organic fruit punch, trying to pretend that it didn't bother either of them that no one had called them over or waved hello or made any indication at all that they were welcome at the event. Schuyler looked around at the cozy groups forming around cocktail tables, smoking on the balcony, or posing for pictures in front of the piano, and realized that, even though she'd known most of these people for almost all of her life, she didn't belong anywhere. It was amazing how even Dylan had managed to find a place for himself, with a popular girlfriend no less, while she and Oliver were just left with each other once again.

"Wanna dance?" Oliver asked, cocking a thumb to the dark room.

She shook her head. "Nah."

"Wanna go instead?" Oliver asked, having come to the same conclusion. "We could go back to The Bank—I bet they're playing better music."

Schuyler was torn. On the one hand, she and Oliver had every right to be there—they were Duchesne students, too—but on the other hand, maybe it was best if they just crept away silently; and maybe with luck no one would even notice they had been there at all.

Oliver's mouth twisted in a strained smile. "This is my fault."

"No—not at all. I wanted to be here," Schuyler protested. "But you're right, we should probably go."

They walked down the grand red-carpeted staircase, where Jack Force was standing on the last step, talking to Kitty Mullins. Schuyler held her breath and walked toward the front door without looking at him. She clutched Oliver's arm tightly.

"Leaving so soon?" Jack called.

She turned around. Kitty Mullins was gone, and Jack was leaning against the banister all by himself. He was wearing a custom French cuffed white shirt, with the front tucked in but the shirttails characteristically hanging out, with crisp khaki pants and a carelessly unbuttoned navy blazer. His tie was askew and he looked nothing less than drop-dead gorgeous. He fiddled with the cuff link on his right wrist.

"We were just about to." She shrugged, smiling in spite of herself.

"Why don't you stay?" Jack asked, smiling back and looking straight into her eyes. "You might have fun."

For a moment, Schuyler forgot Oliver was standing next to her, so when he spoke, she was startled. Oliver looked down at her, his face deliberately blank. "I think I'm going to get another drink. Want to join me?"

Schuyler didn't answer, and for an interminable moment, the three of them stood in an awkward triangle. "I, ah, I'm not thirsty, so I'll catch you later, Ollie. All right?" she pleaded.

Oliver frowned, but he didn't protest, and walked quickly back up the stairs.

Schuyler crossed her arms. What was it about Jack Force? All week after they'd spoken at the funeral, he'd hardly said a word to her, but now he was seeking her out again? Why did she even bother giving him the time of day?

Jack walked up and put an arm around her. "C'mon, let's dance. I think I hear my song."

She allowed herself to be led up the stairs, and this time, heads turned when the crowd spotted the two of them enter the room. Schuyler noted the jealous admiration from the girls, and several guys gave her a respectful glance. She had been invisible just a minute ago, but being in Jack's presence changed all that. He drew her closer, and she swayed to the music. The room was thrumming to the sexy, hypnotic beat of Muse's "Time Is Running Out." *I think I'm drowning, asphyxiated.* . . . She slithered her body next to his, feeling beads of sweat and perspiration on his shirt that the heat between the two of them was generating.

er parents were on their way out. Mimi stood in her bedroom and listened to the sound of her mother's heels on the marble floor, followed by her father's heavier footsteps. "Hi, baby," Trinity called, knocking on her daughter's door. "Daddy and I are leaving."

"Come in," Mimi said. She put her chandelier earrings on and scrutinized her image in the mirror.

Trinity opened the door and stepped inside the room. She was wearing a floor-length gown—Valentino, Mimi thought—and carrying a lush sable wrap around her shoulders. She cut an elegant, glamorous figure, her long blond hair curling around her collarbone. Her mother was often photographed for society columns and fashion magazines.

Her parents were going to some charity ball. They were always out. Mimi couldn't remember the last time either of her parents were home for dinner. Sometimes whole weeks would go by before she would see them. Her mother spent her days in the hair salon, the gym, her therapist's office, or Madison Avenue boutiques; and her father was always at the office, working.

"Don't stay out too late," Trinity admonished, kissing her daughter on the cheek. "You look lovely, by the way. Is that the dress I bought you?"

Mimi nodded.

"A little much with the earrings, though, don't you think?" her mother suggested.

Mimi felt stung. She hated being criticized. "I think they look fine, Mother."

Trinity shrugged.

Mimi noticed her father standing by the doorway, looking impatient. He was talking heatedly on his cell phone. Lately, her father seemed more distracted than usual. Something was bothering him, he was preoccupied and forgetful. The other day she'd arrived home hours after curfew, but her father, who had caught her sneaking in through the kitchen as he was refilling his brandy snifter, didn't say a word.

"Where's Jack?" her mother asked, looking around as if Jack could be hiding under the vanity table.

"Already there," Mimi explained. "My date's running late."

"Well, have fun," Trinity said, patting Mimi's cheek. "Don't get into too much trouble."

"Good night," Charles added, closing the door to her bedroom.

Mimi looked at herself in the mirror again. For some reason, every time her parents bid her good-bye for the evening, she felt bereft. Abandoned. She never got used to it. She removed the chandelier earrings. Her mother was right, they were too much for the dress.

Not long after her parents left, the Italian arrived. He was a distinctly changed man since the day they'd met at Barneys. His cocky demeanor was gone, as was the predatory smile. She'd sucked that out of him. It was Mimi who was in control. She'd almost had her fill of him—he was so easy. No one was a match for her.

"I'll drive," she said, taking the keys from his pocket.

He didn't protest.

It was only a short distance to the American Society, but Mimi ran a few red lights on the way anyway, causing an ambulance to swerve to the side to avoid an accident.

She pulled up to the awning, where the doorman was waiting. They disembarked from the car, and Mimi threw the keys to the valet. The Italian followed her like a puppy. They walked into the mansion together.

Mimi looked devastating in a midnight satin Peter Som dress, with her hair in a high chignon, a triple strand of heirloom South Sea pearls as her only accessory. She tugged on her date's arm and steered him up the stairs. There, she confronted the sight of her best friend, Bliss Llewellyn, in a passionate lip lock with that loser wastoid, Dylan Ward.

"Hellooo." Mimi's voice was icy in the extreme. When did this happen? Mimi didn't like being kept out of the loop.

Bliss disengaged from Dylan's tongue. She blushed when she saw Mimi. Bliss's lipstick was smudged and her hair was askew. Dylan smirked at Mimi.

"Bliss. The bathroom. Now."

Bliss gave Dylan an apologetic look, but she followed Mimi to the ladies' room without question.

Mimi checked the stalls and shooed the maid outside the lavatory. When she was satisfied there was no one inside, she turned to Bliss.

"What the hell is going on with you? You're with *that* guy?" Mimi demanded. "You could be with any guy you want."

"I like him," Bliss said defiantly. "He's cool."

"Cool," Mimi drew out the word so it had ten syllables. Coooooollll.

"What's your problem?" Bliss asked defiantly.

"Problem? I don't have a problem. Who said I had a problem?" Mimi asked, looking around as if surprised to see no one there.

"Is it the Connecticut thing?" Bliss asked. "Because he had nothing to do with it."

"What are you talking about?" Mimi asked.

"I don't know, I heard there was some accident with

some girl in Greenwich, and he was involved." Bliss said. "But anyway, it's not true."

Mimi shrugged. It was the first time she'd heard about it, but it didn't surprise her. "I just don't know why you're wasting your time with him."

"Why do you hate him so much?"

Mimi was taken aback. It was true—she reacted to Dylan with an outsize revulsion. Why did she hate him? She wasn't sure, but she recognized the gut feeling, and her gut was never wrong. There was something she didn't like about that guy, but she couldn't put a finger on it.

"What's up with your boyfriend, by the way? He's like a zombie," Bliss said, pointing to the corner. The Italian heir had followed them inside the ladies' room and was currently drooling on the doorway column. All of Mimi's guys seemed to be like that—brain dead.

"I'll deal with him later."

"I'm going to go back to my date," Bliss said pointedly.

"Fine. But you better be there on Monday for The Committee meeting."

Bliss had almost forgotten. She wasn't even sure she wanted to join some snotty social committee, but she had to appease Mimi somehow. "Sure."

Mimi watched her friend leave. What a waste. It bothered her that Bliss was exerting her independence. There was nothing Mimi disliked more than rebellion in a subordinate. She walked out of the bathroom, tugging on her date's tie to move him forward. And that's when she saw the second image that scorched her brain.

Her brother Jack, on the dance floor, with that Van Alen girl in his arms. Now Mimi really felt like vomiting.

When Schuyler was with Jack, it was like time and space stopped. She didn't even feel like she was in a room full of crowded, sweaty teenagers. They moved with the same rhythm, their bodies perfectly in tune with each other. Jack expertly kept her body close to his, leaning down to breathe lightly on her neck. It was strange how she could see him so clearly in the dark, when everyone else was a shadowy blur. She closed her eyes, and for a moment, saw the two of them—dressed differently. They were in the same ballroom at the mansion, except it was a hundred years earlier—and she was dressed in a long evening dress with a tight corset bodice and silk petticoats, and he was handsome and debonair in a white tuxedo with tails. The music ceased to be the sexy enchantment of the Muse song and became a gentle waltz.

It was like a dream, but it wasn't.

"What's happening?" she asked, looking at him as he twirled her around.

Around them, the ballroom was filled with light and soft music. The tinkling of champagne glasses, the gentle fluttering from the ladies' fans.

But Jack only smiled.

They continued to dance, and Schuyler found that she

knew the intricate steps. At the end of the song, they clapped politely.

Schuyler looked around, and suddenly she was back in the present again, wearing her fifties prom dress, Jack in his blue blazer and red tie. She blinked. Had she imagined it? Was it real? She was confused and disoriented.

"Let's take a break," he said, as he took her hand and steered her off the dance floor. They walked out to the balcony. Jack lit a cigarette. "Want one?"

Schuyler shook her head.

"Did it happen to you too?" she asked.

Jack nodded. He took a puff and exhaled.

They looked out at Park Avenue. Next to Riverside Drive, Schuyler thought it was one of the most beautiful streets in the world. Park Avenue, with its regal array of prewar apartment buildings, fleets of yellow cabs streaming up and down along the median. New York was a magical place.

"What was it?"

But before Jack could reply, there was a scream from inside the mansion. They looked at each other, thinking the same thing. Aggie's death. Was there another? They ran back into the hall.

"It's fine," Mimi Force was saying. "He just passed out. God, get a grip, Kitty." Mimi's Italian date was splayed out on the landing, completely passed out, his face drained of all color. "Jack, a hand?" she snapped, seeing her brother in the doorway.

Jack hurried to his sister's side and helped lug the Italian to a sitting position.

Schuyler could see Jack saying something angrily to Mimi, and she overheard bits of his harangue, "stepped over the line . . . You could have killed him . . . Remember what the Wardens said. . . ."

She stood there, not knowing what to do, when Bliss and Dylan appeared. Dylan took one look at the compromising tableau. "Let me guess, he was with Mimi Force?"

Schuyler nodded. "I think it's time we blow this joint."

"I couldn't agree more," Bliss replied.

Schuyler gave Jack one last look. He was still arguing with his sister. He didn't even notice that she was leaving.

Catherine Carver's Diary
20th of December, 1620
Plymouth, Massachusetts

The men have been gone for days now, and still there is
no word. We are frightened. They should have arrived
there and returned by now, with news of the colony. But
all is silent. The children keep me company and we
make time pass by reading aloud from the books I was
able to bring over. If only we could leave this ship—it is
always wet and terribly crowded, but the structures
are not yet ready. The men are allowed to camp ashore,
but we must remain here, in this dark place.

I am afraid, but I comfort myself with the
knowledge that I will know if John and the rest of the
company are lost. So far, I have not felt nor seen anything
in my visions. There is doubt among the colony as to
whether we have truly escaped. Rumors are spreading
that one of them is here, hidden among us—there is much
whispering and suspicion. The Billington boy has been
missing, they said. Disappeared. Taken. But someone
remembers that he could have gone with the Roanoke
party, so no one is worried, for now. We watch, and wait,
holding our breath.

                                                    —C.C.

SEVENTEEN

Ever since Schuyler could remember, she had spent every Sunday at the hospital. When she was younger, she and her grandmother would take a cab all the way to the uppermost reaches of Manhattan. Schuyler was such a familiar face, the guards never even gave her a visitor's badge anymore but simply waved her through. Now that she was older, Cordelia rarely joined her on the weekly visits, and Schuyler made the trip solo.

She walked past the emergency room, through the glassed-in lobby, and past the giftshop selling balloons and flowers. She bought a newspaper from the stand and walked to the back elevator. Her mother was on the top floor, in a private room that was outfitted like a suite in one of the city's best hotels.

Unlike most people, Schuyler did not find hospitals depressing. She had spent too much of her childhood there, zooming up and down the hallways in a borrowed wheel-chair, playing games of hide and seek with the nurses and orderlies. She ate every Sunday brunch in the basement cafe-teria, where the servers would pile her plate high with bacon, eggs, and waffles.

She passed her mother's regular nurse in the hallway.

"It's a good day," the nurse informed her, smiling.

"Oh. Great." Schuyler smiled back. Her mother had been in a coma for most of Schuyler's life. A few months after giving birth to her, Allegra had suffered an aneurysm and gone into shock. Most days, she lay placidly on the bed, not moving, barely breathing.

But on "good" days, something happened—a flutter underneath the closed eyelids, the movement of her big toe, a twitch in her cheek. Once in a while, her mother sighed for no reason. They were small, infinitesimal signs of a vibrant woman trapped in the cocoon of a living death.

Schuyler remembered the doctor's final prognosis, made almost ten years ago. "All of her organs are function-ing. She is perfectly healthy, except for one thing. Somehow, her mind is closed to her body. She has normal sleep and wake patterns, and she is not brain dead by any means. The neurons are firing. But she remains unconscious. It is a mystery." Surprisingly, the doctors were still convinced there was a chance she could wake up given the right circumstances. "Sometimes, it's a song. Or a voice from the past. Something triggers them, and they wake up. Really, she could wake up at any time."

Certainly, Cordelia believed it was true and encouraged Schuyler to read to Allegra so that her mother would know her voice and perhaps respond to it.

Schuyler said thank you to the nurse and peeked through the small glass window cut in the door so that the nurses could check in on their patients without having to disturb them.

There was a man inside the room.

She kept her hand on the knob, without turning it. She looked through the glass again.

The man was gone.

Schuyler blinked. She swore she had seen a man. A gray-haired man, in a dark suit, kneeling by her mother's bedside, holding her hand, his back turned to the door. His shoulders had been shaking and it looked like he was crying.

But when she looked through the glass again, there was nothing.

This was the second time now. Schuyler wasn't as much troubled as curious. The first time she'd glimpsed him was several months ago, when she'd left the room for a moment to fetch a glass of water. When she'd returned to the room, she was startled to see someone there. Out of the corner of her eye, she'd seen a man standing by the curtains, looking out the window at the Hudson River below. But the moment she had entered, he had disappeared. She hadn't seen his face—just his back and his neat gray hair.

At first, she had been frightened of him, wondering if he was a ghost, or a trick of the light and her imagination. But she had a feeling she knew who the nameless, faceless visitor could be.

She pushed open the door slowly and walked inside the room. She put the thick layers of the Sunday newspaper by the rolling table next to the television.

Her mother was lying on the bed, her hands folded at her stomach. Her fair, blond hair, long and lustrous, was fanned out on the pillow. She was the most beautiful woman Schuyler had ever seen. She had a face like a Renaissance Madonna—serene and peaceful.

Schuyler walked to the chair next to the foot of the bed. She looked around the room again. She peered into the bathroom her mother never used. She pulled back the curtains in front of the window, half expecting to find someone hiding there. Nothing.

Disappointed, Schuyler resumed her spot by the bed.

She opened the Sunday paper. What would she read today? War? Oil crisis? Shootings in the Bronx? An article in the magazine about new, experimental Spanish cuisine? Schuyler decided on the "Styles" section—the "Weddings and Celebrations." Her mother seemed to enjoy those. Sometimes, when Schuyler read her a particularly interesting "Vows" column, her toes wriggled.

Schuyler began to read. "Courtney Wallach married Hamilton Fisher Stevens at the Pierre this afternoon. The bride, thirty-one, a graduate of Harvard and Harvard Business School . . ." She looked hopefully at her mother.

There was no movement from the bed.

Schuyler tried another. "Marjorie Fieldcrest Goldman married Nathan McBride in a ceremony at the Tribeca Rooftop yesterday evening. The bride, twenty-eight, an associate editor at . . ."

Still nothing.

Schuyler searched the announcements. She could never predict what her mother would like. At first, she thought it was news from people they knew, the marriages of heirs and heiresses to old New York families. But just as often, her mother sighed upon hearing a moving story of two computer programmers who had met at a bar in Queens.

Her thoughts drifted back to the mysterious visitor. She looked around the room again, and noticed something. There were flowers by the table. A bouquet of white lilies in a crystal vase. Not the cheap carnations they sold downstairs. This was an exquisite arrangement of tall, glorious blossoms. Their intoxicating smell filled the room. It was funny how she hadn't seen them as soon as she walked in. Who would bring flowers to a comatose woman who wouldn't be able to see them? Who had been there? And where had he gone? More important, where had he come from?

Schuyler wondered if she should mention it to her grandmother. She had kept the stranger's visits a secret, worried that Cordelia would do something to keep the stranger away somehow. She didn't think Cordelia would approve of a strange man visiting her daughter.

She turned the page. "Kathryn Elizabeth DeMenil to Nicholas James Hope the Third." She glanced at her mother's placid face. Nothing. Not even a wrinkle on her cheek. A ghost of a smile.

Schuyler took her mother's cold hand in hers and stroked it. Suddenly, tears rolled silently down her cheeks. It had been a long time since the sight of her mother moved her to tears. But now Schuyler wept openly. The man she'd seen through the glass had been crying as well. The quiet room was filled with a deep piercing grief, and Schuyler wept without abandon for all that she had lost.

EIGHTEEN

*M*onday at school, Oliver gave Schuyler the cold
shoulder. He sat next to Dylan in the cafeteria and
didn't save Schuyler a seat. She waved to the two of them,
but only Dylan waved back. Schuyler ate her sandwich in the
library—but the bread tasted stale in her mouth, dry and
mealy, and she quickly lost her appetite. It didn't help that
even after dancing together on Saturday night, Jack Force
was back to acting like nothing ever happened. He sat
with his friends, hung out with his sister, and basically acted
like his old self. The one who didn't know her, and it hurt.

When school let out, she saw Oliver by the lockers laughing at something Dylan was saying. Dylan gave her a sympathetic glance. "Catch you later, man," Dylan said, patting
Oliver on the back. "Later, Sky."

"Bye, Dylan," she said. The three of them—she, Bliss,
and Dylan, had gone to get slices at Sofia Fabulous Pizza
after the dance. They had looked for Oliver, but he had

already left. He would probably never forgive them for doing something without him. More specifically, he would never forgive *her*. She knew him well enough to understand she had committed a grave betrayal. She was supposed to have followed Oliver up the stairs, but had danced with Jack Force instead. Now he would punish her by taking away his friendship. A friendship she depended on like the sun.

"Hey, Ollie," she said.

Oliver didn't reply. He continued to put his books in his messenger bag without looking at her.

"Ollie, c'mon," she pleaded.

"What?" He shrugged as if he just realized she was standing there.

"What do you mean 'what'? You know what," she said, eyes flashing. Part of her was infuriated with his poor-me act all the time. Like she wasn't even allowed to have any other friends? What kind of friend was that? "You didn't call me all weekend. I thought we were going to go see that movie."

Oliver frowned. "Were we? I don't remember making plans. But then, you know, some people seem to change their plans without telling you about them."

"What do you mean?" she asked.

"Nothing." He shrugged.

"Are you mad at me because of Jack Force?" she demanded. "Because that is really, really, *très* lame."

"Do you like, *like* him or something?" Oliver asked, a stricken look on his face. "That jock loser?"

"He's not a loser!" Schuyler argued. It amazed her how passionately she suddenly felt about Jack Force.

Oliver scowled. He pushed back his cowlick impatiently. "Fine. If that's how you feel, Pod Person." *Invasion of the Body Snatchers* was one of their favorite films. In the movie, conformist aliens replaced all the interesting people. Pod People was what they called their automaton-like peers, who fell into lock step with everything around them: Marc Jacobs handbags! Japanese-straightened hair! Jack Force!

Schuyler felt guilty of something she couldn't even understand. Was it so terrible of her to think Jack Force was a nice person? Okay, so he was a BMOC, the biggest—she had to admit—and yes, okay, so she used to curl her lip at all the Jack Force groupies at school who thought he walked on water. It was just so predictable to like Jack Force. He was smart, handsome, and athletic; he did everything effortlessly. But just because she'd decided to stop disliking him didn't make her some kind of brainless robot did it? Did it? It bothered her that she couldn't decide.

"You're just jealous," she accused.

"Of what?" Oliver's eyes widened, and his face paled.

"I don't know, but you are." She flailed, shrugging her shoulders in frustration. It was always a green-eyed monster issue, wasn't it? She assumed that at some level, Oliver wished he were more like Jack. Adored. Like Jack.

"Right," he said sarcastically. "I'm jealous of his ability to chase a ball with a stick," he sneered.

"Ollie, don't be like that. Please? I really want to talk to you about this, but I have a meeting right now—for The Committee and I . . ."

"You got into The Committee?" Oliver asked incredulously. "*You?*" He looked as if he'd never heard anything so ridiculous in his life.

Was it so far-fetched? Schuyler reddened. So maybe she was nobody, but her family used to be somebodies, and wasn't that what the stupid thing was all about?

But even though she hated to admit it—he had a point. She herself had been mystified as to why she would be chosen for such an honor, although there was that satisfied look on her grandmother's face again—when she'd received the thick white envelope the other afternoon. Cordelia had given her the same appraising glance as when the marks on her arms first appeared. As if she were seeing her granddaughter for the first time. As if she were proud of her.

She hadn't even mentioned it to Oliver, since it was obvious he hadn't gotten one, because he would never keep something like that from her. It struck her as odd that he wasn't chosen to be in The Committee, since his family owned half of the Upper East Side and all of Dutchess County.

"Yeah, funny ha-ha, right?" she said.

His face tightened. The scowl came back. He shook his head. "And you didn't tell me?" he said. "I don't even know who you are anymore."

She watched him walk down the hall, away from her. Each step he took seemed to illustrate the huge gulf that now separated the two of them. He was her best friend. The person she trusted more than anyone in the world. How could he hold joining some dumb social group against her? But she knew why he was angry. Up until now, they had done everything together. But she was invited to The Committee and he was not. Their paths had suddenly diverged. Schuyler thought it was all so silly. She would go to one meeting, just because her grandmother wanted her to, and then drop out. There was certainly nothing about The Committee that was of any interest to her at all.

NINETEEN

t was so funny to see how scared the fresh blood looked. Mimi remembered sitting in that same room last year, thinking they would all start planning the yearly Four Hundred Ball (Theme? Décor? Invites?) and that would be the end of it. Of course, Jack had known something was up, nothing really got past her brother—and apparently, some of them had more of an idea about what was happening to them than others.

Mimi had had the flashbacks too—the memories that would creep up on her without warning. Like the time she'd been in Martha's Vineyard, and instead of being outside the Black Dog, she was outside a farmhouse, wearing some hideous gingham dress—believe it or not. Or the time she was taking her French test and she hadn't studied at all but she aced it, finding that she was suddenly fluent in the language.

She smiled to herself at the memory, and watched as several members of the Senior Committee, her mother among them, entered the room, their Blahnik heels clicking softly on the rose marble floor. There was a hush. The well-coifed women nodded to one another and waved gaily to their children.

The Jefferson Room was the front entry room to the Flood mansion, in the style of Monticello, a tribute to the third president. There was a high, domed cathedral ceiling, several Gainsborough portraits, and in the middle a large round table, where the new members were sitting, looking alternately bored or scared. Mimi didn't recognize all of them, as some were from other schools. God, those Nightingale uniforms were ugly, she thought. The rest of the members of the Junior Committee were sitting on the study desks, or leaning on the windows, or standing with their arms folded, watching silently. She noticed that for once, her brother Jack had deigned to grace them with his presence.

So the Wardens had thought to include the Van Alen girl after all. That was odd. Mimi had no memory of her from her past, not even from Plymouth. She had to have been there somewhere; Mimi just had to dig deeper into her subconscious. When Mimi looked around the room, she could see glimmerings of who everyone else used to be. Katie Sheridan, for instance, had always been a friend—they had "come out" during the 1850 deb season together, and Lissy Harris had been an attendant at her wedding in Newport later that year. But that wasn't the case with Schuyler.

As for Jack, well, they had been together for longer than eternity. His was the only face she ever saw constantly, waiting for her in every incarnation of her past. If Mimi practiced her meditations, perhaps she would be able to access the deepest recesses of her history, back to their creation, in Egypt before the floods.

Mrs. Priscilla Dupont, a regular presence in the city's society pages, and the financial and social force behind many of New York's most august cultural institutions, stepped forward. Like the other women behind her, she was preternaturally slim, with a soft, buttery bob that framed her lineless face. She cut a severe figure in her sharp black Carolina Herrera suit. As committee chair and Chief Warden, she called the meeting to order.

"Welcome to the first meeting of the New York Blood Bank Committee of the season," she said, smiling graciously. "We are very proud to have all of you here."

Mimi zoned out for a bit, barely listening to the standard lecture concerning civil duty and noblesse oblige, enumerating the many services the committee provided their community. The yearly ball, for instance, raised a tremendous amount of money for blood research programs, which was dedicated to the eradication of blood-borne diseases like AIDS and hemophilia. The Committee had founded hospitals and research institutions, and had been instrumental in funding stem-cell research and other advances in medicine.

Then, after the standard spiel, Mrs. Dupont looked intently at the ten young people seated at the table.

"But helping others is not all that The Committee does."

There was an expectant silence.

Mrs. Dupont looked at each student intently before speaking. "You have been gathered here today because you are very special." Her voice had a melodious, cultured quality, soothing and patrician at the same time.

Mimi saw Bliss Llewellyn look uncomfortable. She had given Bliss grief about Dylan, but it was her funeral. Bliss had even threatened to skip the meeting, but somehow Mimi had helped to change her mind.

"Some of you might have noticed certain changes in your bodies. How many have started to see the blue marks on your arms?" she asked.

There was a smattering of hands, a few arms glowing with the sapphire light shining through their skin.

She nodded. "Good. That is the blood beginning to manifest."

Mimi remembered how freaked out she'd been when her marks first appeared. They'd formed an intricate, almost paisley-like pattern up and down from her shoulder to her wrist. Jack had shown her his, and it was another of those things that looked like a coincidence but weren't really—if they held up their arms next to each other's, the patterns matched perfectly.

The blood marks were a map of their personal histories—

it was the blood asserting itself, the Sangre Azul, which marked them as their kind, Mrs. Dupont informed them.

"Some of you find that you are suddenly able to do things very well. Have you noticed that you are excelling in tests you have not studied for? That your memory has become like a photographic snapshot?"

There was more nodding, and some mumbling.

"Has anyone noticed that occasionally, time either slips away or becomes very slow?"

Mimi nodded. That was part of it—the memories that pulled you from the present to the past. You would be walking down a street, minding your own business, and then suddenly you were walking down the same street, but in a totally different time. It was like watching some really cool movie, Mimi thought, except you were starring in it.

"Do you find that you can eat everything and still not gain an ounce?"

There was giggling from some of the girls. A good metabolism, that's what the Red Bloods thought. Mimi had to giggle herself. As if anyone could eat as many cupcakes with whipped cream frosting as they wanted and still be as thin as she was. It was her favorite part of being a Blue Blood. One of the lucky ones. The chosen ones.

"The taste of cooked meat has become unbearable. You have begun to crave things that are raw, bloody."

There were some uncomfortable looks around the table. Bliss looked especially pale. Mimi wondered if anyone had ever experienced what she had—the day she'd devoured several raw, ribeye steaks all by herself; stuffing her face until the blood dripped down her chin and she looked like a mental patient. From the looks around the table, Mimi would bet that had happened to more than a few.

"One last question: how many of you have gotten pets in the last year? Dogs, more specifically?"

Everyone raised their hand. Mimi thought of how she'd found her chow, Pookie, on the beach in the Hamptons one day, and how her brother had gotten Patch on the same evening. Their father had been so proud.

"How many of them are bloodhounds?"

Only Schuyler raised her hand. Mimi grimaced. Her brother Jack had merited a bloodhound too—top level. That was annoying.

"We are here to tell you, you are not to worry. All the things you are experiencing are normal. This is because, like me, like your friends and classmates sitting behind you, like your parents, grandparents, siblings, and relatives, you are part of a long and noble tradition of the Four Hundred."

Mrs. Dupont snapped her fingers and all the lights in the classroom went out. But she, as well as the other committee members, were still glowing. They had an inner light that accentuated their features. It was as if they were made of white translucent marble.

"This is called *illuminata*, it is one of our gifts that aids us in the night and makes us visible to one another."

Some of the students screamed.

"There is nothing to worry about. You are safe here, for we are all the same."

Her voice took on a melodic, hypnotic quality.

"It is all part of the Cycle of Expression. You are the newest Blue Bloods. Today is your induction into your secret history. Welcome to your new life."

The students' faces were lined in shock. Mimi remembered how terrified she'd been, but not because she'd been scared of The Committee—it was a different kind of terror—a more complicated kind of fear. It was the terror of finally knowing the truth. She saw the same fear on the newest members' faces.

They were embarking on a journey into the darkness inside themselves.

TWENTY

*V*ampires?

Were they out of their minds?

The Committee was just a front for a bunch of blood-sucking B-list movie monsters? So they weren't just socialites. They weren't just rich kids. They weren't skinny because they threw up everything they ate. And they weren't fast on the field or incredibly athletic or extraordinarily smart because they were talented; it was because—and this was truly laughable—they were *undead*?

Schuyler had watched the whole thing, half appalled and half fascinated by the cultlike ceremony. Whatever she thought she'd signed up for, it certainly wasn't this. She had to get out of there. She pushed back her chair and was about to leave the room.

But she wavered—and sat back down again. It seemed too rude and against her better judgment. There were so many things they were talking about that made sense. The blue marks on her arms, for instance. Apparently their blood was shining through the skin because it was starting to assert itself, starting to reconnect with all the old knowledge and wisdom and memories of their past lives. Because it was their blood that was *alive*—that was what made them undead—their blood was thousands of years old, from the beginning of time, a living database of their own immortal consciousness. It had a will of its own, and growing up as a Blue Blood meant that you learned how to access and control the vast intelligence that was available inside of you.

Your physical shell expired after a hundred years and then you rested, evolving until they called you up for the next phase in the cycle. Or you could choose not to rest, and instead keep the same physical shell and become Enmortal—like some of the Elders, but you had to be awarded a special dispensation for that. Most Blue Bloods went through the cycle. What did they call it? The three stages of vampire life: Expression, Evolution, Expulsion.

And the bit about the bloodhound—she couldn't argue with that. Beauty had followed her home one day, and it felt like the creature was part of her. Mrs. Dupont explained that their canine familiars were actually a part of their soul that had transferred to the physical world to protect them. The years from fifteen to twenty-one were called the Sunset Years for the Blue Bloods—their most vulnerable time in the cycle of Expression when they shed their human selves for vampire ones. The Blood Manifest, which brought about the memory shock, the dizziness, the sickness, made them weak, and their dogs were their guardians, ministering angels who made sure the Blue Bloods made it to the next phase intact.

Still, it was all just so unbelievable. She'd been convinced that The Committee had been playing a Halloween trick when they lit up like that. Even Jack. So that's why he was all lit up that night at the dance. Why she could see him in the dark.

Wait until she told Oliver!

But, oh. She wasn't supposed to. The Red Bloods—the humans—they couldn't know. Although human familiars—those people whom you performed some Latin thing with—their fancy name for blood-sucking—they could know, but then the ceremony made them forget it or something. There was some kind of hypnotic essence in the process that made them amnesiac, and loyal to the Blue Bloods. Schuyler couldn't imagine wanting to suck anyone's blood. It just seemed gross. But anyway, she had forgotten that she couldn't tell Oliver because he wasn't speaking to her.

Then there were all these rules that governed blood-sucking—like you could only have several human familiars at one time, and you were only allowed to use them once every forty-eight hours. Apparently, life as a vampire wasn't at all like she'd read in books or television, which were just red herrings created by The Conspiracy, a subset of The Committee dedicated to keeping the Red Bloods from knowing their true existence. A Hungarian Blue Blood with a macabre sense of humor had been responsible for the myth of "Count Dracula." The Conspiracy disseminated false information. All those things that were supposed to kill vampires—a crucifix, garlic, the sun—were all just made up. Their idea of a joke.

Because, according to The Committee, nothing could kill vampires. Nothing. Death was merely an illusion.

Schuyler found out the reason Blue Bloods didn't like the crucifix was because it reminded them of their downfall, their banishment from the kingdom of Heaven. (These people were truly deluded, Schuyler thought to herself. They actually thought they were former angels or something. Just what the world needed. More self-aggrandizing rich people.) It turned out garlic was a no-no simply because of the smell. Mrs. Dupont waxed on and on about how Blue Bloods were a very aesthetic-minded race, who favored beauty and harmony above all (and that ruled out Italian food?). And as for sunlight—well, again, it just reminded them of the paradise they'd been expelled from, but most vampires loved the sun—hence the major killer tans on most of The Committee members.

They lived forever, but not as the same person, and not always at the same time. There were only Four Hundred of them at every Cycle. They could ingest food, but most did it out of habit, or simply to be social. Once they reached a certain age, only human blood was needed to keep them recharged. Schuyler found out that taking a human to Full Consumption—draining him or her completely of all blood, effectively killing the human, was the biggest taboo of all. It was the first commandment in the Code of the Vampires— that no harm must come to their human familiars.

Since humans could only take so much blood-letting, most Blue Bloods had several human familiars whom they rotated in their feeding schedule, in the guise of various love affairs. So that was why Mimi had all those boyfriends. It was all part of the Blue Blood lifestyle. And Kitty Mullins—was she one of Jack's human familiars? She had to be, since Kitty wasn't in the assembled group. Schuyler suddenly wasn't very jealous of Kitty Mullins. She felt sorry for her.

The Warden told them that the foremost mission of their kind was to cycle through Expression to evolve into a point where God could forgive them and take them back into heaven again.

Right.

Schuyler didn't believe a word of it. This was someone's sick and not-funny idea of a really stupid prank. She almost expected a reality TV camera crew to pop out of one of the cabinets. But everyone else was muttering, and some of the people next to her were crying with relief.

"I was so worried I was going crazy." She heard Bliss Llewellyn say.

The papers they'd signed to join were also their commitment to the Blue Blood Code. The Code was like the Ten

Commandments of the Blue Bloods—the laws of creation—and they were bound to its rules.

Every Monday they would learn more about their history, as well as how to control their powers. Vampire powers manifested in different ways, the most common were hyper-intelligence and supernatural strength. Most vampires could read human minds, but only the most powerful ones could perform mind-control, the suggestive forcing of their will on a weaker being. A few were shape-shifters who were able to change their physical form at will. The most rare power of all was the ability to stop time, but only one Blue Blood in recorded history had ever been able to demonstrate this power, and had only done so once in all the centuries they had been on earth.

The meetings were also intended to help the younger vampires choose a purpose for that cycle. Schuyler learned that the Blue Bloods were behind the foundation of almost all of the city's most important cultural resources, including the Metropolitan Museum of Art, the Museum of Modern Art, the Frick Collection, the Guggenheim, the New York City Ballet, and the Metropolitan Opera. Blue Bloods sat on the boards, hired curators, and organized fundraisers. It was Blue Blood money that kept all of those wonderful institutions alive.

Mrs. Dupont explained that as they grew older, they would have a chance to serve on all the different committees. Already, the younger generation of Blue Bloods were making an impact, organizing the Save Venice ball, the Young Collectors evenings at the Whitney, and benefits for the High Line, among other worthy causes.

Oh, and of course, they also planned the yearly Four Hundred ball. The biggest social dance of the year, which was held at the St. Regis Hotel Ballroom in December was part of a tradition started during the Gilded Age by a bunch of Blue Bloods. It was called the Patrician Ball then.

But Schuyler didn't believe a word of it. After they were dismissed, several of the newest members huddled, talking to the juniors and seniors to ask more questions. Schuyler walked out quickly by herself. She didn't notice that someone had followed her.

He appeared in front of her without warning.

"Hey." Jack Force smiled. His hair was adorably disheveled as usual. His eyes were green emeralds in his sculpted, handsome face.

"God, how'd you do that?" she demanded.

Jack shrugged. "They'll teach you. It's one of the things we can do."

"Well, 'we' are not going to stick around to find out," she said, elbowing him out of her way.

"Schuyler, wait."

"Why?"

"It's not supposed to happen like this. This meeting was called too early. Usually, this happens in the spring. And by then, almost everyone has figured it out, from the memories. You start to know who you are before anyone has to tell you. The meeting is just a formality. Usually when you're taken into The Committee, you already know."

"Huh?"

"I know it's a lot. It's a lot to handle. But remember what happened Saturday night? When we were waltzing? We saw it because it's happened before. Everything she said in there is true."

Schuyler shook her head. No. She wasn't going to fall for this. They might all be drinking laced Kool-Aid in there, but she had a good head on her shoulders. Things like vampires and past lives and immortality just didn't exist in the real world. And Schuyler was a card-carrying member of the real world. She didn't want to check into CrazyTown any time soon.

"Do this," Jack said, tapping his face, motioning to the side of his jaw.

"Why?"

"You should start feeling them. Right here," he said, pressing a thumb and index finger against each side of his mouth.

"There?"

"Yeah, I know, the Red Bloods think we have them in our front canines, but that's just one more of The Conspiracy's doings. Our wisdom teeth are the ones a bit to the side."

"Wisdom teeth? Like the ones that get taken out at your

dentist?" Schuyler asked, trying not to roll her eyes.

"Oh, I forgot, that's what the Red Bloods call them too. No, not that far back. They stole that term from us, but it doesn't mean the same thing. C'mon, try it. They start appearing right around now."

She rolled her eyes. But she stuck her finger inside her mouth, trying to see if she noticed anything. "Nothing, there's no—Oh." Underneath a small tooth she'd never noticed before, on each side, she felt a sharp point.

"If you concentrate, you can bring them out."

She rolled a finger over them, and pictured the teeth lengthening, coming out of her gums. Amazingly, small sharp enamel fangs began to protrude downward.

"You can learn to extend and retract them."

Schuyler did, her finger tracing the sharp, needlelike end of the tooth. She felt sick to her stomach with an excitement she couldn't control.

Because it was only then that she realized what she had been denying all along.

She was a vampire. Immortal. Dangerous. Her fangs were sharp enough to draw blood—to pierce the skin of a human being. She retracted them slowly, feeling an ache at their disappearance.

She really was one of *them*.

TWENTY-ONE

*O*nce the meeting was adjourned, Bliss was still reeling from everything she'd learned. She was a vampire, or as she corrected herself, a "vam-pyre," which meant fire angel in the Old Tongue, a Blue Blood. One of the undead. So that explained the memories, the nightmares. The voices in her head. It was strange to think of her blood as alive, but that's what they said—that they had all lived before, a long time ago, and were called into service when they were needed. One day they would be in command of all their memories and would learn how to use them.

The knowledge brought a profound feeling of relief. So she wasn't insane. She wasn't losing her mind. What happened at the Met the other afternoon, when she'd blacked out before kissing Dylan, was probably just part of the whole process. That's what Dr. Pat had meant. So she *was* normal. She was *supposed* to feel dizzy and sick. After all, her body was changing, her blood was changing. Maybe now that she understood why she was having them, her nightmares wouldn't scare her as much in the future.

Mimi was grinning from ear to ear when the meeting was over. She walked over to Bliss.

"Are you okay?" she asked gently. She knew it would take some getting used to. But finding out about being a Blue Blood was like a kind of graduation or something. When she and Jack had been inducted, their parents had thrown them a surprise party at the 21 Club.

Bliss nodded.

"C'mon," Mimi said. "Let's go get some steak tartare."

They walked a few blocks toward La Goulue, then took a table on the sidewalk. It was late afternoon, but it was still sunny and warm enough to sit outside. They ordered quickly.

"So, let me get this straight. We can't get killed?" Bliss asked, pulling her seat closer so that no one would overhear their conversation.

"No, we live forever," Mimi said airily.

"Like, forever?" Bliss didn't think she could handle that. How could she live forever exactly. Like, wouldn't she get all wrinkly and stuff?

"Like, forever," Mimi echoed.

"What about the silver stake through the heart?"

"Only if it's from Tiffany's!" Mimi cackled. She took a sip of her Pellegrino. "No, seriously, you've watched too much *Buffy*. There's nothing that can hurt us. But you know Hollywood. They had to think of ways to kill us off somehow. I don't know how we got such a bad rap." She smiled sweetly, a beautiful monster. "It's all created by The Conspiracy, you know. They like to mislead the Red Bloods."

Bliss's head swam. She still felt confused. "But we die after a hundred years?"

"Only the physical shell. If you choose. Your memories last forever, so you're never really dead," Mimi said, clutching the tiny green bottle of sparkling water and taking another gulp.

"What about sucking blood and all that?"

"It's fun," Mimi said, her eyes glazing over dreamily, thinking about her Italian hunk. "Better than sex."

Bliss blushed.

"Don't be such a prude. I've had tons of humans."

"You're like a vampire slut," Bliss joked.

Mimi's face darkened, but then she saw the humor in it. "Yeah, a real vamp, that's me."

Their food arrived—rare pink slices of tuna carpaccio for Mimi and a mound of steak tartare soaked in a raw egg for Bliss.

Bliss thanked whoever made eating uncooked beef not only acceptable but fashionable and dug into her entrée. She wondered how Dylan would feel if she wanted to make *him* her human familiar. Did she just, you know, start necking and then chomp on him?

The tables on the sidewalk were quickly filling up with diners from the surrounding neighborhood, mostly women in chic leather and suede coats and pristine denim trousers, holding bulging shopping bags from Madison Avenue stores, stopping by for a quick reprieve from an exhausting day of trying on clothes. Bliss looked around. Almost every table was picking at similarly uncooked foods. She wondered how many of them were Blue Bloods. Maybe all of them?

"What about the sun? Doesn't it like, kill us?" she asked, between bites. The steak melted on her tongue, cold and tart.

"Are you shriveling up and dying right now?" Mimi snickered. "All of us go to Palm Beach every Christmas. Hello!"

Bliss had to admit she wasn't. Dying, that is, from sun exposure. But she did get itchy, and told Mimi about that.

"You just have to see Dr. Pat. There's a pill you take if you're allergic. Some of us are; it's genetic. But you're lucky, the pill you get, it clears acne too. Isn't that great?"

Mimi put down her fork, wiped her lips with a napkin, then took out a Tweezerman file and began sharpening her back teeth with it.

"It's good for the fangs," she matter-of-factly informed Bliss.

Bliss was disconcerted. For a moment, she had looked past the Mimi sitting there and into the face of a person whom she felt she used to know.

"It happened, huh?"

"What?"

"You saw me. Or, you know, some version of me, in some past life of yours."

"Is that what it was?"

"Who was I?" Mimi asked, curious.

"Don't you know?"

Mimi sighed. "Not really. You can go into meditation and learn about your whole history, but it's kind of a pain. You don't really need to."

"You were getting married," Bliss said. "You were wearing a crown."

"Mmmm." Mimi smiled. "I wonder when that was. I don't remember that one. I've been married in Boston, Newport, and Southampton—the one in England, not Long Island. That's where we're from, you know. At least, until we came here. I remember when we settled Plymouth, do you? That's how far back I can go. For now."

But Bliss didn't tell Mimi that in her memory, she'd seen Mimi kissing her groom passionately. And that groom looked an awful lot like her brother, Jack. It was just too creepy. Maybe there was some kind of Blue Blood explanation for it, but for now, Bliss would keep the disturbing image to herself.

ordelia had asked Schuyler to meet her for tea in the St. Regis lobby after school. She was waiting for her at their usual table when Schuyler arrived. Her grandmother was sitting in the middle of a bright, beautiful room, Schuyler's bloodhound resting at her feet. The St. Regis didn't usually allow pets in the dining room, but they made an exception for Cordelia. After all, the Astor Court was named after Cordelia's great-grandmother.

Schuyler walked up to her, feeling a mixture of anger and apprehension.

Her grandmother sat serenely, her arms folded on her lap. She looked vibrant and energetic. Her skin glowed, and her hair was a pale, platinum blond, with just a hint of the lightest silver. For the first time, Schuyler noticed that her grandmother always looked like this after her weekly treatment at Jorge's. But now she wondered—was the flamboyant

South American merely her hairdresser? Or one of Cordelia's human familiars? Schuyler decided she didn't want to know.

"May I be the first to offer congratulations," Cordelia said.

"I don't know what I'm supposed to be so happy about," Schuyler replied.

Cordelia motioned to the chair across from her. "Sit down, granddaughter. We have much to talk about." A tuxedoed waiter approached, and Cordelia ordered the three-course tea service. "Chinese Flowers for me, please," Cordelia decided, closing the menu.

Schuyler sat down, and Beauty nestled her head on Schuyler's lap. Schuyler patted her dog absently, wondering if Beauty were really her guardian angel, or just a stray dog that she'd found on the street. She took a cursory glance at the leather-bound menu and paged through it. "Earl Grey is fine for me, thanks."

"Why didn't you tell me before?" Schuyler demanded, when the waiter had left.

"It is not our way," Cordelia said simply. "The burden of knowing oneself shouldn't be cast until you are ready. And we have found Priscilla does an excellent job with the induction ceremony."

Priscilla Dupont. The Chief Warden. Committee Chair. Socialite. Whatever she really was.

"Cordelia, how old are you exactly?" Schuyler asked.

Cordelia smiled. A rueful, knowing smile. "You have guessed correctly. I have gone beyond the usual cycle. I am tiring of this Expression. But I have my reasons for staying."

"Because of my mother . . ." Schuyler said. It dawned on her that Cordelia had been allowed to live longer so that she could take care of her, since her mother was . . . what was her mother doing exactly? If she was an all-powerful vampire, then why was she in a coma?

Her grandmother looked pained. "Yes. Your mother has made some terrible choices."

"Why? Why is she in a coma? If she's invulnerable, why won't she wake up?"

"That is not for me to discuss," Cordelia said sharply. "Whatever she has done, you should count yourself privileged to have her heritage."

Schuyler wanted to ask her grandmother what she meant by that, but the waiter had arrived bearing a silver three-story tray laden with scones, sandwiches, and petit fours. Shiny silver teapots filled with brewing tea were placed next to their porcelain cups.

Schuyler hastened to pour and was admonished by her grandmother. "The strainer."

She nodded and placed the silver tea-leaf catcher on top of her cup. The waiter took the teapot and poured the hot tea into the cup. The pleasant aroma of steeped bergamot filled her senses. She smiled. Ever since she was a little girl, she'd enjoyed the afternoon ritual. In the background, the harpist was playing a gentle melody.

For a few moments, nothing was said as she and her grandmother helped themselves to the treats. Schuyler put a lavish spoonful of Devonshire cream on a scone and topped it off with a dollop of lemon curd. She took a bite, murmuring her delight.

Cordelia dabbed her napkin on her mouth. She chose a small finger sandwich filled with crab salad, took a tiny bite, then put it back on her plate.

Schuyler discovered she was starving. She took a sandwich—a thin, square cucumber one, and another scone.

The waiter silently refilled the top two levels of their tray, gliding in unobtrusively.

"What did you mean by lucky?" she asked her grandmother. She was confused. It sounded like she'd had some sort of choice for being who she was, but from all she learned at the meeting, being a Blue Blood was her destiny.

Cordelia shrugged. She lifted the lid of her teapot and frowned at the waiter who was standing quietly against the wall. "I'd like some more hot water please," she said.

"Are you really my grandmother?" Schuyler asked, between bites of the smoked salmon on rye.

Cordelia smiled again. It was disconcerting, as if a curtain had been raised and Schuyler was finally allowed a real peek at the old woman.

"Technically, no. You are wise to discern that. There have been Four Hundred of us since the beginning of time.

We do not have progeny in the traditional sense. As you have learned, through the cycles, many are called but some choose to rest. More and more of us are resting, slumbering, choosing not to evolve and staying in the primal state. When our bodies expire, all that is left is a single drop of blood with our DNA pattern, and when it is time to release a new spirit, those of us who choose to carry are implanted with the new life. So in a way, we are all related, but we are not related at all. But you are my charge and my responsibility."

Schuyler was bewildered by her grandmother's words. What exactly did she mean by that? "And my father?" she asked tentatively, thinking of the tall man in the dark suit who visited her mother.

"Your father is of no concern to you," Cordelia replied coldly. "Think no more of him. He was not worthy of your mother."

"But who . . . ?" Schuyler had never known her father. She knew his name: Stephen Chase, and that he was an artist who had met her mother at his gallery opening. But that was all. She knew nothing of her father's family.

"Enough. He is gone, that is all you need to know. I told you, he died soon after you were born," Cordelia said. She reached over and smoothed her granddaughter's hair. It was the first time Cordelia had shown Schuyler physical affection in a very long time.

Schuyler reached for a strawberry tart. She felt deflated and uneasy, as if Cordelia wasn't telling her everything.

"It is a hard time for us, you see," Cordelia explained as she surveyed the plate of petit fours and chose a hazelnut cookie. "There are less and less of us who are choosing to go through the proper cycles, and our values, our way of life, is quickly disappearing. Not many of us are adhering to The Code anymore. There is corruption and dissent in the ranks. Many fear that we will never reach the exalted state. Instead, there are those who choose to fade away into the darkness that threatens to take us. Immortality is a curse and a blessing. I have lived too long already. I remember too much." Cordelia took a long sip from her teacup, her pinky finger pointed down daintily.

As Cordelia put down her cup, her face changed. It sagged and withered in front of Schuyler's eyes. Schuyler felt a wave of sympathy for the old woman, vampire or not.

"What do you mean?"

"It is a coarse time we live in. Full of vulgarity and despair. We have tried our best to influence, to show the way. We are creatures of beauty and light, but the Red Bloods no longer listen to us. We have become irrelevant. There are too many of them now, and too few of us. It is their will that will change this world, not ours."

"What do you mean? Charles Force is the richest and most powerful man in the city, and Bliss's father is a senator. They're both Blue Bloods, aren't they?" Schuyler asked.

"Charles Force," Cordelia said grimly as she stirred honey into her tea. She released her teaspoon with such anger, the other patrons looked up at the sound. Her face was set. "He has his own agenda. As for Senator Llewellyn, holding political office is a direct violation of our Code. We do not interfere directly with human political affairs. But times have changed. Look at his wife," Cordelia said, with a hint of distaste. "There is nothing Blue Blood about her taste and clothing—'downwardly aspirational,' I believe it's called." She sighed as Schuyler rested her hands on hers. "You are a good girl. I have told you too much already. But perhaps it will help when you realize the truth one day. But not now."

It was all Cordelia would say on the matter.

They finished their tea in silence. Schuyler ate a bite out of a chocolate éclair, but put it down on her plate without finishing it. After everything Cordelia had told her, she was no longer hungry.

TWENTY-THREE

*I*t was maddening how your best friend could twist the knobs inside of you so much that it hurt. Oliver had known just where to stab his little barbs. Pod Person indeed! What about him, with his Vespa and his one-hundred-dollar haircuts? And his yearly birthday parties on board his family's two-hundred-foot yacht? Wasn't that just another stab at the popularity that eluded him?

Ever since The Committee meeting and the tea with Cordelia, Schuyler felt uprooted, unmoored, on unsteady ground. There was so much her grandmother had confirmed about their past—and so much she had still left out. Why was her mother in a coma? What had happened to her father? Schuyler felt more lost than ever, especially since Oliver had stopped speaking to her. They had never argued about anything before—they used to joke that they were just two halves of the same person. They liked all of the same things (50 Cent, sci-fi movies, pastrami sandwiches slathered with mustard) and disliked all of the same things (Eminem, pretentious Academy Award fodder, self-righteous vegetarians). But now that Schuyler had moved Jack from the "Not" to the "Hot" column, without campaigning for Oliver's approval, he had cut her off.

The rest of the week passed by without incident, Cordelia left for her annual fall sojourn on The Vineyard, Oliver continued to refuse to even acknowledge her existence, and she hadn't had a chance to talk to Jack again. But for once, she was too busy with real-world concerns—passing biology, getting her homework done, turning in her English essays—to deal with either of them.

Her jaw hurt whenever she extended and retracted her fangs, and she was relieved to find she didn't feel that deep-set hunger yet. She learned from her grandmother that the *Caerimonia Osculor*, the Sacred Kiss, was a very special ceremony, and most Blue Bloods waited until the age of consent (eighteen) to perform it; although incidents of pre-term sucking were rising with every generation—some vampires were even as young as fourteen or fifteen when they took their first human familiar. Taking a Red Blood without his or her consent was also against The Code.

On a whim, she decided to visit her mother at the hospital that Friday afternoon after school, since Oliver hadn't invited her to come over and hang out at his place as usual. Besides, she had a plan, and she didn't want to wait until

Sunday to try it out. Instead of reading from the newspaper like she did every week, she was going to ask her mother some questions instead. Even if her mother couldn't answer her, Schuyler would feel better just getting them off her chest.

The hospital was quieter on a weekday afternoon. There weren't as many visitors in the lobby, and there was a desolate, abandoned feeling to the building. Life was lived elsewhere; even the nurses looked anxious to take off for the weekend.

Schuyler looked through the glass again before stepping inside her mother's room. Just as before, there, by the foot of the bed, was the same gray-haired man. He was saying something to her mother. Schuyler pressed her ear against the door.

"Forgive me . . . forgive me . . . wake up, please, let me help you. . . ."

Schuyler watched and listened. She knew who it was. It had to be him. Schuyler felt her heart beat in excitement.

The man kept talking. "You have punished me long enough, you have punished yourself long enough. Return to me. I beg."

Her mother's nurse appeared at her elbow. "Hi, Schuyler, what are you doing? Why don't you go inside?" she asked.

"Don't you see him?" Schuyler whispered, indicating the glass.

"See who?" The nurse asked, puzzled. "I don't see anybody."

Schuyler pressed her lips together. So only she could see the stranger. It was as she thought, and she felt a flutter of anticipation. "You don't?"

The nurse shook her head and looked at Schuyler as if there were something slightly wrong with her.

"Yeah, it's just a trick of the light," Schuyler said. "I thought I saw something. . . ."

The nurse nodded and walked away.

Schuyler entered the room. The mysterious visitor had disappeared, but Schuyler noticed that the chair was still warm. She looked around the room and began to call out softly, the first time she had done so since she had spotted the crying stranger.

"Dad?" Schuyler whispered, walking into the next room, a fully furnished living room suite for guests, and looked around. "Dad? Is that you? Are you there?"

There was no answer, and the man did not reappear. Schuyler sat down on the chair he had vacated.

"I want to know about my father," Schuyler said to the silent woman in the bed. "Stephen Chase. Who was he? What did he do to you? What happened? Is he still alive? Does he come visit you? Was he here, just now?" She raised her voice, so that if the visitor was still within earshot, he would hear her. So that her father would know that she knew it was him. She wished he would stay and talk to her.

Cordelia had always given her the impression that her father had done some grievous harm to her mother. That he had never loved her—a fact that she could not reconcile with the image of the sobbing man by her mother's bed.

"Mom, I need your help," Schuyler pleaded. "Cordelia says you can get up anytime you want, but you won't.

"Wake up, Mom. Wake up for me.

"Please."

But the woman on the bed didn't move. There was no reply.

"Stephen Chase. Your husband. He died when I was born. Or so Cordelia tells me. Is that true? Is my father dead? Mother? Please. I need to know."

Not even a toe wiggle. Not even a sigh.

Schuyler gave up her questions and picked up the newspaper again. She continued to read the wedding announcements, feeling oddly comforted by the litany of marital unions and their homogeneity. When she had read every single one, she stood up and kissed her mother on the cheek.

Allegra's skin was cold and waxy to the touch.

Like touching death.

Schuyler left, more disheartened than ever.

TWENTY-FOUR

*T*hat evening, when Schuyler returned home, she received an interesting phone call from Linda Farnsworth.

Stitched for Civilization was the hottest jeans company in the city (and de facto the world) at the moment. Their splashy billboards were all over Times Square, and their three-hundred-dollar signature "Social Lies" cut—super-low-rise, butt-lifting, thigh-shaping, whiskered, stained, bleached, torn, and extra-long—were the cult object of obsession among the *jeanerati*. And apparently, the designer had flipped for Schuyler's moody Polaroid.

"You are the new face of Civilization!" Linda Farnsworth gushed on Schuyler's cell phone. "They must have you! Don't make me beg!"

"Okay, I guess." Schuyler said, still feeling a bit dazed by Linda's exuberance.

Since Schuyler couldn't come up with a legitimate

reason to deny the fashion gods (who was she to say no to Civilization?), the next morning she journeyed downtown for the scheduled photo shoot. The photo studio in far west Chelsea was housed in a mammoth block-long building that had formerly been a printing factory. The service elevator was manned by a bleary-eyed gentleman in a utility suit, who had to manually operate the lift to take Schuyler to the proper floor.

She walked down a maze of hallways, noting the many designer names and Web site addresses that looked familiar on the nameplates of the closed doors.

The photo studio was in the northeast corner. The door was propped open and loud, electronic music was blasting from the inside.

She walked inside, not quite sure what to expect. The studio was a large, open space, an all-white box with shiny white polyurethaned floors and floor-to-ceiling windows. A white "seamless" background was carved into one wall, and a tripod was set up across from it. Yawning interns were wheeling in clothing racks so that a dreadlocked stylist could examine the garments.

"Schuyler!" A scrawny man with a five o'clock shadow, wearing a shrunken T-shirt and baggy jeans, approached her, holding a hand out enthusiastically. He was smoking and wearing Ray Ban aviator sunglasses.

"Hey," Schuyler said.

"Jonas Jones, remember me?" he asked, lifting his sunglasses and grinning.

"Oh . . . of course!" Schuyler said, a little intimidated. Jonas Jones was one of Duchesne's most notorious alums. He had graduated a few years ago. He had made a big splash in the art world with his shredded paintings. He had also done a movie, *Lumberjack Quadrille*, that had placed at Sundance, and his latest career turn was as a fashion photographer.

"Thanks so much for doing this," he said. "I'm sorry it's so last minute. But that's the biz." He introduced Civilization's designer, a former fit model with rock-hard abs and protruding pelvic bones.

"I'm Anka," she said cheerfully. "Sorry to get you up so early on a Saturday. But it's going to be a long day. It'll be okay, though. We have tons of doughnuts." She motioned to the buffet table laden with green-and-white Krispy Kreme boxes.

Schuyler liked her already.

"All right. Let's get you in hair and makeup," Jonas declared, pointing Schuyler toward a corner where a dressing-room mirror framed with two rows of incandescent bulbs was set up in front of two canvas-backed high chairs.

Bliss Llewellyn was sitting in one of the chairs. Linda had failed to mention that there were *two* faces of Civilization that year. The tall girl was already made up. Her hair had been teased into a large bouffant, and her lips were painted cherry red. She was wearing a fluffy white robe and chatting on her cell phone. Bliss gaily waved a manicured hand in Schuyler's direction.

Schuyler waved back. She hauled herself into the chair, and a British makeup artist who introduced herself as Perfection Smith began to assess the condition of her skin. At the same time, a dour hairstylist grabbed chunks of her hair to examine it, clucking his tongue in disapproval.

"Late night?" Perfection inquired, holding up Schuyler's chin to the light. "You're very dry, luv," she said in a nasal cockney accent.

"I guess," Schuyler said. She hadn't been sleeping much since The Committee meeting. It spooked her to think that while she slept, her own blood was waking up, seeping into her consciousness, and all the memories and voices of her past lives were clamoring for control of her brain. Even though Jack had explained it didn't work that way—the memories were your memories, so they were part of you, and there was nothing to be scared about—Schuyler wasn't so sure.

She closed her eyes as her face was rubbed, pinched, prodded, buffed, powdered, and slathered; and her hair was pulled, brushed, and blow-dried, almost singeing her roots.

"Ow!" she yelped, as the hair dryer came dangerously close to burning her scalp. But the grumpy hair stylist didn't even apologize.

She was also having trouble following all the directions Perfection was barking at her. Schuyler had never realized getting her makeup done would be this hard. She had to do so many things, sometimes at the same time, so that the makeup artist could do her job correctly. Perfection was like a drill sergeant. "Open. Wider. Look to the side. Look to the other side. Look at my knee. Look at the ceiling. Close your mouth. Rub your lips together. Look at me. Look at my knee."

Schuyler was exhausted by the time her transformation was finished.

"Are you ready?" Perfection asked. She wheeled the chair around so Schuyler could finally see herself in the mirror.

Schuyler couldn't believe what she saw. It was the face of her mother staring back at her. The face that smiled serenely from the wedding photos Schuyler kept underneath her bed. She was as gorgeous as a goddess.

"Oh," Schuyler said, her eyes wide. Until now, she had never known she looked like her mother.

God, she was *really* pretty, Bliss thought. *Pretty* wasn't even the word—that would be like calling Audrey Hepburn good-looking. Schuyler was *transcendent*. Why hadn't she ever noticed that before? Bliss wondered. She was talking to Dylan on her cell—telling him about the house party she was hosting later that night—her mom was going to DC to visit her dad, and Jordan was going to sleepover at a friend's. She was telling him what time to arrive when she noticed Schuyler's transformation.

Schuyler looked every inch a model. Her lips were full and glossy. They had blown out her black-blue hair so that it hung, straight and perfect as an ebony curtain, down her smooth back. The stylist had put her in a pair of tight Stitched for Civilization jeans; and underneath all those hobo layers, Bliss noticed that Schuyler had a great little figure, slim and waifish. Bliss suddenly felt like a horse next to her.

"Talk to you later, they're calling us on set," she told Dylan, folding up her phone.

"God, you look so great," Bliss whispered, when they were lined up next to each other against the white backdrop.

"Thanks," Schuyler said. "I feel so silly." She had never worn so little clothing in public before, and was trying not to feel too self-conscious about it. They were both wearing the jeans, and the jeans only—their backs were to the camera, and they were both covering their chests with folded arms, even though the stylist had pasted nude-colored Band-Aids on their breasts to cover their nipples. She had agreed to model mostly out of curiosity, a social experiment she could analyze later, but she had to admit, it was also pretty fun.

It was cold in the studio, and Jonas was yelling instructions to everyone over the Black Eyed Peas blasting from the overhead speakers. There was a frenzied atmosphere of jittery assistants and lighting technicians jumping at the photographer's every word. Bliss and Schuyler were attacked with hair spray canisters whenever there was a break. A deadpan seriousness prevailed as Jonas and Anka heatedly discussed issues such as whether their hair should be blowing in the wind or not (sexy or clichéd?), or if the jeans looked better from the front or the side.

The girls posed and pouted, trying not to blink at the flash of the camera. Suddenly feeling inspired, Bliss pulled Schuyler closer for a tight embrace.

"Twisted," Jonas smirked from behind the lens.

During their lunch break, they put their robes back on and huddled with the crew around the buffet table, piling their plates with vegetables and seared tuna. (Rare, thank God, Bliss thought.)

"Smoke?" Jonas asked, taking a crumpled pack of cigarettes from his back pocket. "C'mon girls, join me."

They put down their plates and followed him and Anka out to the balcony.

"So, you both go to Duchesne?" Anka asked, taking out a long menthol cigarette and breathing in as Jonas lit it with his Zippo.

"Uh-huh," Bliss nodded, accepting a somewhat squashed Camel from Jonas.

Schuyler shook her head. Cigarettes made her ill. She was just out there for the company and the view. The balcony overlooked the abandoned railway flats next to the river. A barge was slowly making its way across the water. Schuyler looked out happily. She would never get tired of looking at the city.

"I went to Kent," Anka volunteered. "I met Jonas at RISD."

Jonas nodded. "We've been collaborating ever since." He blew out a smoke ring. "We're so glad we found you girls. We really wanted our kind to be the face of the campaign."

"Our kind?" Schuyler asked.

Anka laughed, and flashed her fangs at them.

"You're Blue Bloods!" Bliss gasped.

"Of course." Jonas nodded, amused. "Most people in fashion are. Haven't you noticed?"

"How can you tell?"

"You just know—in the shape of the eyes and a certain overall bone structure," Jonas explained. "Plus, we're also really, really picky. Just look at Brannon Frost, the editor-in-chief of *Chic*. Hello."

"She's a vampire?" Bliss goggled. But then, it made so much sense—the frail figure, the dark oversized sunglasses, the pale skin, the rigorous dedication to perfection.

"Who else?" Schuyler asked.

Jonas rattled off several more names: a popular "bad-boy" designer who had recently revitalized the goth-grunge look, a model who was the current face of a lingerie company, an acclaimed makeup artist who popularized blue nail polish. "There are tons," he said, tossing his cigarette off the balcony.

They changed the subject when several people from the crew came out to join them, and Jonas started to tell a series of raunchy jokes that only Perfection could match in grossness. Schuyler laughed with all the rest, feeling like she and

Bliss were part of an ad hoc, slightly deranged family.

"Why isn't Mimi here?" Schuyler asked suddenly. It didn't make sense that she would have this experience while Mimi, who thrived on this kind of attention, had been left out.

Bliss suddenly laughed. She'd completely forgotten about Mimi. Mimi would die when she heard that Bliss and Schuyler had been chosen for the Stitched for Civilization campaign and not her!

"Yeah, where is Mimi?" Bliss asked.

Jonas scratched his head. Schuyler noticed the faded blue marks on his arms. "Mimi Force? We considered her for like, a second. Remember, Ank? What happened with her?"

"Linda told me her day rate," Anka said. "Apparently when she signed up, she told Linda she wouldn't get out of bed for less than ten thousand dollars a day. Sorry, girls, but without any experience, that's just not realistic. I didn't even make an offer. Besides, we wanted you two."

"I guess sleep is just too important to her." Bliss smirked. "She doesn't know what she's missing." Bliss gave Schuyler one of her rare, genuine smiles.

"Right." Schuyler nodded.

Schuyler smiled back. She was starting to like Bliss Llewellyn even more.

They went back to the shoot, draping themselves over each other, and when Jonas shouted, "Fire! Fire! Give me fire!" they practically burned the lens.

hey let her keep the jeans! Schuyler was thrilled.
The shoot ended late, way past the six o'clock end time,
and by the time they were done it was dark outside. She said
her good-byes in a flurry of air kisses, waving madly to everyone at the corner. The merry gang dispersed—Anka and the
stylists disappearing in a Town Car, the hair and makeup
crew into taxicabs, Jonas and his assistants to the nearest bar.

"Do you want a ride uptown?" Bliss asked. "My driver
should be here shortly."

Schuyler shook her head. "Thanks, but no. I think I'm
going to walk a bit." It was a nice night, cloudless and brisk.

Bliss shrugged. She was already sucking on a cigarette,
and in her tight T-shirt, new jeans, and purple monkey-fur
jacket, she looked every inch an off-duty model. "Suit yourself. Don't forget, *mi casa*, tonight at ten."

Schuyler nodded. She hugged the plastic bag with her

new jeans tightly. She was back to wearing her many layers—a black T-shirt over a black turtleneck over a black jersey skirt over a pair of gray jeans and white-and-black striped stockings, with her beat-up black combat boots. She meant to walk east toward Seventh Avenue, and continue to stroll up through Times Square, Lincoln Center, and the Upper West Side on the way home.

As she walked east toward Tenth Avenue, she felt a little wary. The streets were completely deserted; the warehouse buildings that housed new art galleries were dark and forbidding. The streetlights flickered and there were puddles on the ground from a recent rainstorm. Schuyler suddenly wished she had taken Bliss up on the offer of a ride. Feeling anxious, she began walking faster toward the well-lit avenues. If she could only get to Ninth, with its coffeeshops and boutiques, she knew she would be safe.

She tried to shake the fear off, thinking it was merely paranoia from the dark—and who was she to be afraid of the dark anyway? She was a vampire! She laughed ghoulishly, but she felt a prickle of fear just the same.

She couldn't deny it anymore.

Someone was following her.

Or some thing . . .

She broke out into a quick run, her heart beating wildly in her chest, and her breath coming in quick gasps. She turned around. . . .

A shadow against a wall.

Her shadow.

She blinked. Nothing. There was nothing and no one. You're just paranoid, you're just paranoid, she told herself. She forced herself to walk slower, to show herself she wasn't afraid.

Only a few more steps to the haven of Ninth Avenue . . . so close . . . she turned around one more time . . . and felt something reach around and grab her by the neck. She struggled to breathe, to open her eyes, to kick away, but she couldn't scream; it was as if something had locked her throat and was squeezing it tightly. A dark, giant creature . . . tall and strong as a man, a dense and noxious presence with . . . crimson eyes, crimson eyes with silver pupils shining in the dark, staring at her . . . boring into her brain . . . and then she felt it. . . .

No! No! No!

She refused to believe it, but yes, there were fangs pricking her skin—but how could it be? She was one of them! What was this?

With all the strength she had, she pushed back at her attacker—but she flailed, scratching at nothing—it was like the wind had her in its grip—it was no use, the fangs came down—stabbing her neck—her blood, her bright blue blood, seeping the life out of her. . . . She was dizzy and confused . . . she was going to pass out—when a blue-black blur suddenly materialized, barking madly.

Beauty!

The bloodhound snarled and leaped at the dark creature. The monster released her, and Schuyler staggered onto the dirty sidewalk, clutching the side of her neck. Her bloodhound ran in circles, snarling and barking loudly. The dark creature disappeared.

Beauty was still barking when Schuyler finally opened her eyes. Someone was holding her up.

"Are you okay?" Bliss Llewellyn asked.

"I don't know," Schuyler said, still in shock. She tried to regain her balance, leaning heavily on Bliss's shoulder, her legs still shaking.

"Easy," Bliss soothed.

Beauty was still barking, with loud, angry howls, and growling at Bliss.

"Heel, Beauty, heel, that's Bliss, she's my friend," Schuyler said, putting an arm out to soothe the trembling dog. But the dog wouldn't stop. Beauty ran around Bliss, nipping her ankles.

"Ouch!"

"Beauty, that's enough!" Schuyler said, taking Beauty's collar roughly. Where had she come from? How had she known? Schuyler looked into the dog's intelligent black eyes. You saved me, she thought.

"What happened?" Bliss asked again.

"I don't know. I was just walking when something attacked me from behind. . . ."

"I heard you," Bliss said, her voice shaking. "I was

waiting over there, outside the studio, for my car, when I heard you screaming down the block, so I ran over to help."

Schuyler nodded, still dazed from the experience. Her bag and its contents were scattered around her—her books open and soaking in the puddles, her prized new jeans crumpled in a heap.

"What do you think it was?" Bliss asked, helping Schuyler gather her things and putting them back in her leather bag.

"I don't know . . . it seemed . . . unreal," Schuyler stammered. She zipped up her bag and shouldered it roughly. She was still a bit unsteady on her feet, but holding Beauty's leash made her feel better somehow. She felt stronger around the bloodhound, more substantial.

Already, the memory of the attack was staring to fade— a dark mass, with shining red eyes and silver pupils—and teeth, teeth sharp enough to puncture skin—fangs—just like hers—but when her fingers touched the side of her neck, there was nothing there anymore. Not a wound. Not even a scratch.

Catherine Carver's Diary
23rd of December, 1620
Plymouth, Massachusetts

Alas! Alas! Everyone from Roanoke is
disappeared. Myles and the men found
nothing of the colony. The shelters had been
dismantled, the animals nowhere in sight. There
was nothing but a bare patch of field. Nothing
remained of the settlement except for a lone sign
nailed to a tree. John showed it to me.

CROATAN

It chilled my blood to see it. Alas! Alas! It is
true. We are cursed! They are here. All is lost!
We weep for our kindred. But we must protect the
children. We are not safe!

-C.C.

TWENTY-SIX

*R*idiculous. It was one of Mimi's favorite words. Her python Birkin? Ridiculous! Her father's new G-5 jet? Ridiculous! Bliss Llwellyn's house party? OTT, baby. Ridiculous to the max. There was nothing like a party to get her blood flowing. Mimi surveyed the crowded room. Almost everyone from The Committee was there, and a great selection of delicious-looking Red Bloods. She was glad she'd convinced Bliss to throw the party.

Things had been way too serious around school—what with midterms just around the corner, the seniors stressing about applications, the lingering sadness from Aggie's funeral— and they all needed to relax. Bliss had been hesitant at first— badgering Mimi with a thousand petty concerns like, *Will anyone show? What about food? Who's going to buy the beer? What about the furniture? What if something happens to it? Some of it is really expensive!* She had almost driven Mimi mad with all her angst-ing. "Leave it all in my capable hands," Mimi finally told her friend.

So, in quick succession, Mimi commandeered an army of publicists and event planners to transform the Llewellyns' triplex penthouse apartment into a bacchanalian haven— complete with a sponsored open bar (as if alcohol had any effect on them anyway), a crew of models holding serving trays bearing bite-size edibles (potatoes stuffed with caviar, lobster timbale, and shrimp cocktail), and slew of brightly colored goodie bags stuffed with a full line of luxurious bath products. Mimi had even hired a crew of reflexologists, aromatherapists, and Swedish masseurs to give foot, hand, and back massages to the guests. The white-clad "pamper police" were busy at work kneading, chopping, and relieving the stressed-out muscles of the private school elite.

Bliss arrived home to find all the furniture on the downstairs floor replaced with zebra-pint couches, shag rugs, and Aero lamps. A DJ was setting up in front of the fireplace.

"Don't freak, okay?" Mimi said, holding up a hand in front of Bliss's face.

"What the f—?" Bliss asked, looking around at the total transformation of her parents' home into a groovy '60s-style nightclub.

Mimi explained she'd had all of Bliss's parents' things secured and transferred to a storage location, and that everything would be put back tomorrow morning before they got home. She'd gotten the idea from one of the design magazines, suggesting an empty house was the perfect place for a party.

"Am I a genius or what? This way, you don't have to worry about anything being stolen or broken," Mimi assured. "Where have you been, anyway? You're late!"

Bliss shook her head, aghast. She wondered what her stepmother would say if she knew everything in her precious Penthouse des Rêves was in Jersey somewhere. She gaped at Mimi for a second, threw her hands up in resignation, and headed to her room to change.

"You're welcome!" Mimi called.

The latest smashcut remix (Destiny's Child vs. Nirvana) was blasting from the Llewellyns' surround-sound stereo system. Mimi smiled to herself in the dark. She wet her lips, which shone brightly with blood. Her Italian boyfriend was somewhere, passed out as usual.

"Lychee martini?" a waitress asked, offering her a cocktail.

The perfect chaser. Mimi smiled and emptied its contents. Then she took another and another, while the confused server just stared at her.

"Thirsty?" a voice behind her asked.

Mimi turned around.

Dylan Ward was watching her, his dark hair masking his eyes. The same feeling of dread came over her. "What's it to you?" she sneered.

Dylan shrugged.

Mimi walked over to him. She was wearing a cropped red leather Dsquared jacket and a vented chiffon Balenciaga skirt that hugged her curves. It annoyed her that Dylan didn't even notice how good her legs looked in that skirt. There was something impudent about that. As if he didn't even care what she looked like. Blasphemy! She checked his neck. So far, no sign that Bliss had tried to seal their bond. Mimi smiled to herself. An idea formed in her head. Now, this could be fun.

If she performed the *Caerimonia Osculor* on Dylan before Bliss did, he would be bound to her forever. He would forget all about Bliss. That would serve Bliss right for continuing to see him after Mimi had forbade her to do so. Not that she was even interested in Dylan or anything, she was just bored.

She lowered her lashes flirtatiously. "Help me with something?" she asked, leading him away from the party.

In the shadows, she looked like a helpless beautiful girl, and without even thinking about it, Dylan found himself automatically following her farther and farther, deeper into the dark.

"But she invited me! I know the owner of this apartment!" Schuyler argued. She'd never even heard of a guest list for a house party. But then again, she'd never been invited to one. The elevator had opened to the lowest floor of the apartment, and Schuyler found her way barred by a cadre of stony-faced PR girls.

"Did you RSVP?" one of them demanded, snapping her gum and looking balefully at Schuyler's mismatched outfit. She was wearing a flowing tunic with layers of plastic beads, denim shorts over black leggings, and scuffed cowboy boots.

"I only heard about it today," Schuyler groaned.

"I'm sorry, you're not on the list," the clipboard girl replied, savoring the rejection.

Schuyler was about to step back into the elevator and go home, when Bliss appeared from behind a hidden doorway.

"Bliss!" Schuyler cried. "They won't let me in."

Bliss marched over. She had showered and changed into a slim-fitting Missoni dress with zigzagging stripes and high-heeled gladiator sandals. She took Schuyler by the arm and pulled her through the PR barricade, over the protests of the clipboard hellions. She led Schuyler into the main room, which was crowded with Duchesne kids angling for drinks at the bar, sprawling on couches, or dirty-dancing by the windows.

"Thanks," Schuyler said.

"Sorry about that. It's Mimi. I told her my parents were away and I was thinking of hosting a little get-together, and she puts together like, the MTV Movie Awards After Party."

Schuyler laughed. She looked around—there were go-go boys and go-go girls writhing in cages hung from the ceiling, and she recognized several famous faces in the mix. "Isn't that——?" Schuyler asked, noticing a peppy teen actress funneling beers in front of a cheering crowd.

"Yeah," Bliss sighed. "C'mon, let me show you the rest of the place. It doesn't usually look like this."

"I'd love to—but I have to do something first."

Bliss raised her eyebrow. "Oh?"

"I have to find Jack Force."

She had to find Jack. She had to tell him what had happened to her. They had barely spoken to each other since the night of the Informals, but she perceived he was the only one who would understand. She was fighting to hold on to the memory—already it was slipping—already she couldn't remember the exact details of where, why, or how it had happened—except for the eyes, eyes glimmering red in the dark, with silver pupils. Red eyes and sharp teeth.

But the Llewellyns' penthouse was like a house that magically expanded—everywhere you turned, there were rooms and rooms off innumerable hallways, with hidden treasures. Schuyler found an indoor lap pool, a fully equipped gym, and what looked to be a staffed day spa on the premises, complete with massage tables and essential oils, as well as a game room filled with old-fashioned carnival arcade toys, with mechanical fortune tellers and penny games, all of them in perfect working condition. She pushed a penny into a slot and removed her fortune.

YOU ARE A TRAVELER AT HEART.

MANY JOURNEYS AWAIT YOU.

She wished Oliver were there to see it.

"Have you seen Jack? Jack Force?" she asked everyone she bumped into.

She was told that he had just left, or was on another floor, or had just arrived. He seemed to be everywhere and nowhere.

At last, she found him in an empty guest bedroom on the uppermost floor. He was strumming a guitar and singing softly to himself. Downstairs was the house party of the century, but Jack preferred the silence upstairs.

"Schuyler?" he said, without looking up.

"Something happened," she said, closing the door behind her softly. Now that she'd finally found him, all the feelings she'd bottled up came out. She was trembling, so scared that she hadn't even noticed that he'd divined her presence from sense alone. Her eyes were wide and frightened. Without thinking twice, she ran to his side and sat next to him on the bed.

He put an arm around her protectively. "What's wrong?"

"I was at a photo shoot today, and afterward, I was walking alone . . . and I was . . . I can't remember. . . ." She struggled for the words. For the images. At the time, they were burned into her brain, yet it felt like she was grasping—reaching for them. She held on to the tendrils of the memory—something terrible had almost happened to her—but what? What words could convey what had happened, and why was her memory betraying her?

"I was attacked," she forced herself to say.

"What?" He cursed. He shook her shoulders, then held her close. "By whom? Tell me."

"I don't remember. It's gone, but it was . . . powerful, I couldn't stop it. Red . . . red eyes . . . teeth . . . going to suck . . . here," she said, pointing to her neck. "I felt it, deep into my veins . . . but look, I don't have any puncture wounds? I don't understand."

Jack frowned. He kept his arms around her. "I'm going to tell you something. Something important."

Schuyler nodded.

"Something is hunting us. There is something out there hunting Blue Bloods," he said softly. "I wasn't sure before, but I am now."

"What do you mean, hunting *us*? Don't you have it backward? We're the ones everyone else needs to be afraid of!"

Jack shook his head. "I know it doesn't make sense."

"Because The Committee said we can't be kil—"

"Exactly," Jack interrupted. "They've always told us we live forever, that we're immortal and invulnerable, that nothing can kill us, right?" he asked.

Schuyler nodded. "That's what I was telling you."

"And they're right. I've tried."

"Tried what?"

"I've jumped in front of trains. I've cut myself. I was the one who fell out the library window last year."

Schuyler remembered that rumor—how some kid had jumped off the third-floor balcony and landed in the cortile. But she hadn't believed it. No one could survive a fifty-foot jump and live, much less land on their feet.

"Why?"

"To see if what they were telling us was true."

"But you could have died!"

"No. I couldn't. The Committee was right about that, at least."

"That night—that night in front of Block 122—you *were* hit by the taxi."

He nodded. "But it didn't hurt me."

"No." Schuyler nodded. So she had seen him fall underneath the taxicab's wheels. He should have died. But he had appeared on the sidewalk, whole. She'd thought she was just tired from the night, that her eyes were strained. But it had actually happened. She'd seen it.

"Schuyler, listen to me. Nothing can harm us . . . except—"

"Except . . . ?"

"I don't know!" He folded his hands into fists in frustration. "But there *is* something out there. The Committee isn't telling us everything."

Jack explained that before the first meeting, the senior members of The Committee decided that they wouldn't tell the premature about the danger. That instead of warning everyone, it was best to leave them in the dark for now. It was enough that they would find out about their true heritage first; no reason to raise alarm bells where there might be none. Except that he hadn't believed them. He knew they were keeping something from them.

"They're holding something back. I think it's something that might have happened before, in our history. Something to do with Plymouth, when we first came here. I've tried to dig it up, but it's as if it's blocked from my sight. When I try to think about it, all I remember is a word. A message nailed to a tree in an empty field. It contained one word: *Croatan*."

"What's that?" *Croatan*. Schuyler shuddered, repulsed by the mere sound of it.

"I have no idea." Jack shook his head. "I don't even know what it is. It could be anything. It might be a place, I'm not sure. But I think it has to do with what they haven't told us about. Something with the power to kill Blue Bloods."

"But how do you know? How can you be so sure?" she asked him, alarmed.

"Because, like I told you, Aggie Carondolet was murdered," he said, looking intently into her deep blue eyes.

Schuyler was silent. "And?"

"Aggie was a vampire."

Schuyler gasped. Of course! That's why she'd felt so empathic at the funeral. She'd known, somehow, that Aggie was one of them.

"She's never coming back. She's gone. Her blood—all of it—was drained from her body. Her memories, her lives, her soul—gone. Sucked out, just like we suck the Red Bloods," he said sadly. "Extinguished. Taken."

Schuyler looked at him in horror. It couldn't be true.

"And she wasn't the first. This has happened before."

Catherine Carver's Diary
25th of December, 1620
Plymouth, Massachusetts

Panic everywhere. Half of us are determined to flee,
to find safer ground. Perhaps head south, farther
away. The Conclave is meeting today to discuss the
alternatives. John is convinced that one of them is hidden
here among us, that one of us has succumbed to their
power. He is determined to convince the Elders.
William White will stand with him, he said. But
Myles Standish is adamant about staying. He has
argued that there is no proof, even if the Roanoke
colony is gone, that they were overtaken by Croatan. A
hysterical lie, he says, perhaps even a willful
misleading. He will not believe messages left on trees.
The Conclave is ever in accordance, it has never happened
that they have failed to reach an agreement. It is not
our way to doubt. Myles Standish has led us well for
as long as I can remember. But John is certain there is
danger. Stay or flee? But where would we go?
                                    — C.C.

hat was up with the dry ice? It was like a bad magic show in there. Bliss shooed away some freshmen helping themselves to more than one goodie bag on the exit table, and circled the room. She felt a rising panic. She couldn't find Dylan anywhere. The one guy she wanted to see, and he was missing.

She flopped down on the leather couch and looked at the hallway leading to the massage rooms. Two people were making out behind the ice sculpture. The taller figure looked familiar—that worn, beaten leather sleeve, the fringes of that white silk scarf—it had to be . . .

"Dylan?" Bliss asked.

Mimi turned around. Shit. She should have taken him into the bathroom or somewhere more private. She retracted her fangs quickly and put on her most dazzling smile.

"Bliss, sweetie. There you are," she said.

Dylan turned around, his eyes glassy and unfocused.

"What are you doing?" Bliss asked Mimi.

"Nothing." Mimi shrugged. "We were just talking."

Bliss pulled Dylan out of the shadowy corner. She checked his neck for marks, but there were none. Good. She glared at Mimi and led him away.

"What were you doing with her?" Bliss demanded.

Dylan shrugged. He hadn't even realized he was with Mimi Force. He'd been lost in a daze, as if he were under a spell. He blinked his eyes and looked at Bliss. "Where have you been?" he asked, his voice suddenly normal.

"Looking for you," she said.

He smiled.

"C'mon, I want to show you my room," Bliss said.

Dylan looked strange in the confines of her bedroom. It was as if he were too male, too dirty . . . too real. He smirked at her white princess bed with the fluffy floral comforter, at the pale green rug, the pink wallpaper, the white wicker armoire, the four-story dollhouse, the theater lights on her vanity table.

"Okay, I know. It's a little girlie," she conceded.

"A little?" he teased.

"It's not me. It's my stepmother. She thinks I'm still like, twelve or something."

Dylan grinned. He shut the door softly and dimmed the lights.

Bliss suddenly felt nervous. "Excuse me for a sec," she said, slipping into the bathroom to catch her breath.

It was going to be her first time, and she was a little scared about it. She was going to do it—IT—the *Caerimonia Osculor*—that would bind him to her in blood—she was going to give him the Sacred Kiss—but he didn't know it yet. Apparently, you just started doing it—and they—the humans—they would begin to writhe in ecstasy and it would all be hot and sweaty and—and afterward she would feel better than she'd ever felt before.

When she walked out, Dylan was already lying on the bed, his back against the fluffy down pillows. He looked skinny and sexy in his ripped Ben Folds T-shirt. He kicked off his Nike Dunks and patted the empty space next to him.

Bliss found his scarf and leather jacket hanging on the bedpost, and it gave her an idea. She slipped a duplicate of her keys in the pocket.

"What are you doing?" Dylan asked.

"Nothing—just giving you something that will maybe make it easier for us to get together next time," Bliss said coyly.

"Well, get over here *now*."

"I'm cold," she said, slipping under the covers.

After a second, Dylan pulled aside the covers and slid in beside her.

They lay there for a while, listening to the sound of gangsta rap thumping from the second floor.

"You are really cold," he marveled.

"But your skin's warm," she said.

He wrapped his arms around her. They started kissing— and Bliss was thankful she didn't black out this time, as she felt his hand explore underneath her dress, reaching for her bra. She smiled, thinking boys were all alike. He would get what he wanted, but not before she got what she wanted.

She closed her eyes, feeling his warm hands unclasp the hook of her bra. He pulled her dress off, over her head. She raised herself a little off the bed to help him, and then she was lying there, in only her Cosabella thong, before him.

She opened her eyes to see him hovering over her. She pulled him closer.

He made a cross of his arms and pulled his T-shirt over his chest. He was so skinny she could feel the ribs underneath his skin. They were both breathing quickly, and in a moment, he was lying on top of her, pushing his body against hers.

She caressed his neck and felt the hard bump underneath his jeans pressing against her thigh. She rolled over him, so that she was on top of his chest. He held her close, his hands caressing her back, slipping off her underwear. She began kissing his mouth, the line of his jaw, licking her way down.

She felt her back teeth extend; she was going to do it— Now! She could almost smell his thick, rich blood—she raised her jaw, and suddenly, the room was ablaze with light.

"What the hell?" Dylan poked his head out of the comforter.

Two giggly sophomores were standing in the hallway, watching them.

"Oops!"

Bliss looked up at them, her fangs still sticking out.

The two girls at the door screamed.

Bliss quickly disarmed. Shit. The Committee had warned them about this—they couldn't allow the Red Bloods to see them as they were, to know their real nature. They were just some kids. Maybe they'll think they were just imagining things.

There was a loud thump from behind her. Dylan had fallen off the bed and was rolling heavily to the floor.

Still underneath the comforter, Bliss turned and saw what had made him jump. Her father was standing in the hallway. Where had he come from? How had they gotten home so early? Bliss scrambled to put her dress back on.

"What's going on in here?" the senator asked. "Bliss, are you all right? And who are you?" he asked.

Dylan was hopping around, zipping up his jeans and pulling down his T-shirt. He grabbed his leather jacket and stuffed his feet back into his sneakers. "Uh, nice meeting you, too."

"What is the meaning of this?" Forsyth Llewellyn demanded. "Bliss, who was that boy?"

With a sinking heart, she heard Dylan's quick footsteps stomp down the stairs.

He'd never be hers now.

"Young lady, are you going to explain? What exactly is going on in here? And what happened to all of our furniture?"

chuyler didn't doubt that what Jack had told her was true. He told her about the way they'd found Aggie at the club, with all her blood drained, just like a Red Blood after full consumption, except it had happened to one of their own. Just as they preyed on the humans, something was preying on them. Jack explained that while the Blue Bloods kept to The Code—there hadn't been a human death due to blood-sucking in centuries, those that hunted the Blue Bloods were not as chivalrous.

Then he told her about some girl who'd died in Connecticut over the summer. Another Blue Blood. She had been a Hotchkiss sophomore, and they'd found her in the same condition as Aggie. There was also a sixteen-year-old Choate boy who'd died just before school had started. He'd been in The Committee as well. Again, the blood was drained completely from his body. Aggie's death was just the latest one they knew about.

Jack was certain the Elders were hiding something from them, and he was determined to find out what it was. "Why do I feel like I've seen this before, like I've lived this before? But there's something blocking my memory. Almost as if someone's tampered with it somehow. But we need to know. We need to know what's happening to us. And why everyone who's dying is our age. Are you with me?" he asked.

Schuyler nodded.

"We need to find out how to stop it. For all our sakes. We can't live in the dark, like we are now. The Elders think it will just go away, but what if it doesn't? I want to be prepared for it—whatever it is."

He looked so passionate and angry, Schuyler couldn't help but put a hand on his cheek. He looked at her intently. "It's going to be dangerous. I don't want to drag you into something you might regret."

"I don't care," Schuyler said. "I agree with you. We have to find out what this thing is. And why it's preying on us."

He pulled her closer to him, and she felt his heart beating in his chest. It was amazing how calm and centered she felt—like this was the only place in the world where she belonged.

He leaned over, his nose gently brushing hers, and she tilted her chin up to be kissed.

When their lips met, and their tongues touched, it was like they were kissing in a hundred different places, and her senses were flooded with new sensations and old memories.

He kissed her, and their souls melted into each other in a melody older than time.

"What a pretty picture."

Schuyler and Jack pulled away.

Mimi Force was standing in front of them, clapping her hands slowly.

"Mimi, there's no need for that," Jack said coldly.

Schuyler blushed. Why on earth was Jack's sister staring at her like that—like, like, like she was jealous of them! How creepy and weird was that? Was she missing something here? Mimi was his twin sister.

"The Llewellyns are here. They're pretty pissed. I came to warn you. We gotta scram."

Jack and Schuyler followed Mimi to the back staircase, where dozens of kids from the party were already streaming out, carrying their goodie bags and chattering excitedly.

"Damn! I forgot to take one!" Mimi cursed. "And I'm out of body lotion, too," she lamented as they walked out to the lobby. The building's concierge looked a tad horrified to encounter a rash of teenagers bursting through, some still carrying beer bottles and cocktail glasses. He gazed openmouthed at the sight of them.

The group dispersed, and Mimi ran out to the street, where their car was waiting. "Jack, are you coming?" she asked, turning around impatiently.

"You're leaving?" Schuyler asked.

"For now. I'll explain later, okay?" he said, taking

her hand and giving it a squeeze. Then he let go.

Schuyler shook her head. No. Why did he have to go? She wanted him to stay by her side, not run off again somewhere without her. Her lips still ached with the force of his kiss, her cheeks red from his stubble.

"Don't be like that. Remember what I said. Be careful. Don't go anywhere without Beauty."

She nodded mutely, and was about to turn away. Then, as if she thought better of it, she reached out and grabbed his arm. "Jack."

"Yes?"

"I . . ." she faltered. She knew what she wanted to tell him, but she couldn't bring herself to say the words.

It turned out she didn't have to. Jack put a hand on his heart and nodded. "I feel the same way about you."

Then he turned around and disappeared inside the black Town Car that was carrying his twin.

chuyler watched the car pull away, conflicting feelings and thoughts warring in her brain. Aggie was a
vampire—and she was dead—which meant she, Schuyler,
could die too. She'd almost died that day—if not for Beauty.
She watched the car disappear around the corner. He was
leaving her. Something about the way he had walked away
made her feel as if he were walking away from her forever,
and she would always be alone.

"Miss, can I help you?" the disgruntled concierge asked,
pursing his thin lips.

Schuyler looked around. She was the only person standing in the Llewellyns' marble lobby. "Actually, yes," she replied
smoothly. "I need a taxi, please."

The doorman at the front soon sent her on her way.

"Houston and Essex, please," she instructed the driver.
She was going to the only place where she knew she would
find a safe haven.

* * *

The line at The Bank was long as usual, but this time Schuyler walked straight up to the front of the rope. "Excuse me," she told the drag queen, "but I really need to get inside right now."

The Cher wannabe pursed her lips. "And I really need a tummy tuck. But nobody gets what they want. Get in the back like everyone else."

"You don't understand. I said, LET ME IN RIGHT NOW." The words were a roar in her mind, even stronger than the last time she had tried it.

The drag queen staggered back, holding her head as if she'd received a blow. She nodded to the door goons, who lifted the rope.

Schuyler strode in, mentally waving away the ticket taker and the ID check who were thrown backward toward the wall as if they were just dominos.

Inside the club was pitch-black, and Schuyler could barely make out the shadowy forms of revelers swaying, humming and dancing to the intoxicating music. The music was so loud, she could hear it in every pore of her body. She felt rather than saw her way through the crowd, slowly but steadily pushing her way forward through the mass of dancers. Finally, she found the stairs that led up to the lounge on the top floor.

"Grass, crank, blow," came the hiss of a reptilian drug dealer perched on the third step. "Something for the little lady? Take her to the stars?"

Schuyler shook her head and hurried past him.

She found Oliver on the second level, next to the windows, sitting cross-legged and admiring the view of Avenue A. He looked at once aloof and perfectly miserable. She felt exactly the same way. She didn't realize how much she'd missed him until she saw his familiar face, his hazel eyes hidden underneath his long bangs.

"Well, well. To what do I owe this honor?" he asked, when he noticed her standing in front of him. He pushed his hair out of his eyes and stared at her in a hostile fashion.

"I have to tell you something," she said.

Oliver crossed his arms. "What is it? Can't you see I'm busy?" he snapped, motioning to the large empty space surrounding him. "Well, I *was* busy," he muttered. "There were *tons* of people here just a minute ago. I don't know how you missed them."

"Just because . . ." she protested. *Just because I left you at the dance alone and went to be with another guy*, she had begun to say, but she stopped herself right in time. She *had* left Oliver alone, and for all intents and purposes, she had been his date at the Informals. He was her best friend, and she saw him all the time, but at the dance, they were supposed to have been a couple. Not in a romantic way, but in a, we're-here-at-this-crappy-dance-together-so-let's-make-the-best-of-it kind of way. What she'd done was incredibly rude. How would she feel if Oliver had done the same to her? If he'd left her alone, with no one to talk to, while he went off and danced with Mimi Force? She would probably give him as cold a shoulder as he was giving her now. Colder, most likely.

"Ollie, I'm sorry about last Saturday night," she said finally.

"What's that?"

"I'm sorry. I said I'm sorry. Okay? I wasn't thinking."

He looked up at the ceiling, as if talking to an unseen observer. "Schuyler Van Alen, admitting she was wrong. I don't believe it." But his hazel eyes were crinkling, and she knew they were friends again.

That was all she'd had to say. Sorry.

No matter how overused and abused it was, *sorry* was still a powerful word. Powerful enough to make her best friend talk to her again.

"So we're okay?"

Oliver had to laugh. "Yeah. I guess."

Schuyler smiled. She sat down on the ledge next to him. He was her best friend, her confidante, her soul mate, and in the past week, she had ignored and neglected him, pulling away because she was too frightened to tell him the truth about herself. "I have to tell you something about *me*." She reached out and took his hands in hers. "Oliver, I'm a . . . I'm a vam . . ."

Oliver's face softened. "I already know."

"Excuse me?" she demanded.

"Schuyler. Let me show you something."

* * *

Still holding her hand, he led her down past the basement pit and the coed bathrooms toward the corner where she had encountered that strange blank wall the last time they were at the club. He muttered a few words, and an outline of a door glowed brightly. Oliver pushed softly on it, and the wall swung open, revealing steep, curving stairs that led to the lowest bowels of the building.

"What is this?" Schuyler asked as they stepped through the entryway. The wall shut behind them, leaving them alone in the dark.

Oliver removed a thin flashlight from his shirt pocket. "Follow me," he said. They began to walk down the stairs, which spiraled down for what seemed like miles. Schuyler was out of breath by the time they arrived at the bottommost stair.

There was another door, a more magnificent one this time, made of gold, ebony, and platinum. *INGREDIOR PERCIPIO ANIMUS* read the inscription around the perimeter.

Oliver removed a gold key from his wallet and twisted it in the lock.

"Where are we? What is this all about?" Schuyler asked, stepping tentatively inside the room.

It was a library—a large, airy space that smelled like chalk dust and parchment. There were bookshelves that reached seventy-five feet to the ceiling, and a maze of ladders and bridges that connected the towering stacks. It was bright and well-lit, and decorated with cozy Aubusson rugs and bankers lamps. Several scholars at rolltop desks looked up curiously when they entered. Oliver bowed to them and led Schuyler to a private cubicle.

"This is the Repository of History. We keep it protected."

"Who's *we*?"

Oliver put a hand to his lips. He led her to a small, shabby desk in the back of the room. It held a gleaming iBook, several framed photographs, and a dozen Post-it notes. He searched the shelf on top of the desk and made a satisfied sound as he took down a book, musty and dirty from years of use. He blew softly on the cover. He flipped to the first page and displayed it to her. He pointed to the crumbling page where a family tree was illustrated, the name Van Alen inscribed in the center, with Hazard-Perry in small letters underneath.

"What is this?"

"It's how we're related," Oliver explained. "How we're associated, I mean. We're not family, so don't worry."

"What do you mean?" she asked, still trying to fathom the fact that there was a secret library underneath the nightclub.

"My family has served yours for centuries."

"Come again?"

"I'm a Conduit. Like everyone in my family. We've been caretakers for the Blue Bloods forever. We work as doctors, lawyers, accountants, financiers. We've served the Van Alens in that capacity since the 1700s. You know Dr. Pat? She's my aunt."

"What do you mean, *serve* us? Your family is so much richer than mine," Schuyler pointed out.

"An accident of fate. We offered to ameliorate the situation, but your grandmother wouldn't hear of it. 'Times have changed,' she said."

"But what does that mean—a Conduit?"

"It means, we serve a different purpose. Not all humans are familiars."

"You know about that?" she asked. She looked down at the page again, recognizing the names of her ancestors on her mother's side.

"I know enough."

"But why didn't you ever say anything?"

"I'm not allowed."

"But how come you can know what you are, but I didn't know what I was?"

"Search me. That's how it's been since the beginning. Being a Conduit is something that's passed down, that's taught, and it's easier to teach at a young age. We serve to keep the Blue Bloods a secret, to protect them and help them manage in the real world. The practice is an old one, and only a few vampire families keep Conduits nowadays. Most got rid of theirs, like the Forces. It's an ancient tradition, and some Blue Bloods don't keep to the old ways anymore. Like your grandmother said, things are different now. I'm one of the last of our kind."

"Why?"

"Who knows?" Oliver shrugged. "Most Blue Bloods can

take care of themselves anyway. They don't need us anymore. They don't trust the Red Bloods to help; they want to
control them instead."

There was a commotion at another desk, and they
turned to see a cowering, hunchbacked librarian being
berated by an angry older woman with a distinctly recogniz-
able blond bob.

"What's happening?"

"Anders is getting it again. Mrs. Dupont is not happy
with the way his research is going."

Schuyler recognized the graceful figure of The
Committee chair. "And Anders is?"

"A librarian. All the library staff is Red Blood. Conduits
who don't work for any single family anymore."

Schuyler noticed that the Blue Bloods at the library
ordered the librarians around with a grand, authoritative
fashion, and for a moment she was embarrassed to be a vampire. What happened to common courtesy?

"Why do they talk to you guys like that?"

"Your family never did," Oliver said, blushing. "But like
I told you, most Blue Bloods resent us. They don't even think
we should be here, or know about them. But no one from
your side wants to take over the Repository. No one's interested in caretaking some old books."

"What's she doing here anyway?" Schuyler wondered,
watching Mrs. Dupont look through some paperwork her
Conduit had brought.

"This is the headquarters of the Conclave of Elders. The Wardens—you know. They meet over there, in the board-room behind the stacks."

"How long have you known? About me, I mean." Schuyler asked. She looked back at his desk, at the photograph of the two of them that had been taken the past summer in Nantucket. Oliver, his face red from the sun, was squinting at the camera. He had a dark, deep caramel tan and his hair had lightened to a rich golden brown, while Schuyler looked pale and uncomfortable, underneath a huge floppy beach hat, a white smudge of sunscreen on her nose. They had looked so young then, even if it was only a few months ago. Last summer they had been just kids—just a bunch of kids who were dreading going back to high school. They had spent the two weeks sailing and making bonfires on the beach. To Schuyler it felt like a lifetime ago.

"I've known since I was born. I was assigned to you," he said simply.

"You were *assigned* to me?"

"As I understand it, every member of a vampire family is assigned a human conduit at birth. I'm two months younger than you. You could even say you're the reason why I was born. I sought you out. Remember?"

Schuyler looked back on all her memories. She remembered now how he kept making friendly overtures, and how she'd resisted at first. He was always sitting next to her in class, or asking her questions, and finally, in the second grade, when they'd shared that dismal lettuce sandwich, they'd become friends.

"And what exactly do you do?"

"I help you. I nudge you in a certain direction, suggest how to use your powers so you can discover them on your own. Remember that night at The Bank, when I kept telling you 'think positive and we'll get in'?"

She nodded. It was as she suspected, and she told him how she had used it this evening to get past the drag queen at the door.

He guffawed. "Priceless. Wish I'd seen that one."

She smiled wryly. "Well, they did tell us at Committee meetings that mind-control was possible."

"But only very few vampires can do it," he pointed out.

"I don't get it, though. If this Repository is down here— why were you so worried about us not getting into The Bank? Surely there's another entrance to this place."

Oliver nodded. "There is. Through Block 122. That's why they have a 'members-only' policy. As in, Blue Bloods and their guests only. I could have gone in through there, I'm one of the few with a key—even though I'm only a lowly Red Blood—but I hate that place."

She nodded for him to continue.

"The Bank is a fluke. For the longest time it was empty. But then a couple of neighbors and homeless people reported seeing people go in and never coming out, and to alleviate suspicion, they figured they'd rent out the top floors to anyone interested. This club promoter came along first, and they liked the idea of a nightclub so much they decided to open another club next door—but a private one of course."

Schuyler processed all the information. The private night-club, The Committee, it certainly fit in with everything she knew about the Blue Bloods so far. They liked to keep to themselves.

She was still bothered by Oliver's admission, however, and his explanation for their friendship. She couldn't help but remember how Oliver was always loaning her money, and she never had enough to repay him, but he never seemed to worry about it, or ask for it back. Was that part of it? Where did the Conduit end and her friend begin?

"So anyway, you're not really my best friend? You're like, my babysitter?"

Oliver laughed and raked a hand through his thick hair. "You can call me whatever you want. You're just not going to get rid of me that easily."

"Then why did you get so mad at me when I told you about The Committee?"

He sighed in frustration. "I don't know—I guess a part of me didn't want it to be true, even though I knew it was. I mean, I knew it would happen, but I just wanted us to be the same, you know? And we're not. I'm a Red Blood. You're immortal. I guess it just bummed me out. So sue me, I'm human." He smiled at his pun.

"You're wrong. Apparently I'm not so immortal, actually," Schuyler said.

"What do you mean?"

"Jack told me that something is killing vampires."

"That's impossible." Oliver shook his head. "I told you, there's something wrong with that dude." He cracked a smile.

"No, there's not. I'm serious. It's a secret. Aggie was a vampire. And she's not recycling. She's gone. She's dead. Like, *really* dead this time. Her blood is gone."

"Oh, God," Oliver said, his face draining of color. "I didn't know. That's why I told you I wasn't in mourning at her funeral. I thought, what's the big deal? She'll just come back."

"She's never coming back. And she's not the only one. There have been more—other kids are getting killed. Blue Bloods. We're not supposed to die, but we are."

"So what does Jack want to do about it? What does he know?" Oliver asked.

"He wants to find out what's hunting us." She told him about Jack's memory about Plymouth. The message nailed to a tree in a lonely field. Croatan.

"How is he going to do that?" Oliver asked.

"I don't know, but I think we can help him."

"How?"

Schuyler looked around the old room.

"This library holds the entire history of the Blue Bloods, right? Maybe there's something in here we can find."

THIRTY

*T*hey had invaded the sanctuary. Ever since Mimi could remember, her father retreated into his book-lined den after work and hardly ever came out for dinner. It was a locked door, a special place, where children weren't allowed. Mimi recalled scratching at the door when she was a child, desperate for his attention and love, only to have her nanny cart her away, with admonishments and threats. "Leave your father alone, he's a busy, busy man with no time for you."

Her mother had been the same way—a distant satellite—always on vacation somewhere children were not allowed or welcomed. It had been a lonely, quiet childhood, but she and Jack had made the most of it. They were each other's sole company; they depended on each other to the point where Mimi didn't know where she ended and her brother began. Which made what she was about to do even more necessary. He had to know the truth.

She strode into the great marble hallway and walked right up to the locked door to their father's study. With a wave of her hand, the lock disintegrated and the door blew open with a bang.

Charles Force was sitting at his desk, nursing a crystal goblet of dark red liquid. "Impressive," he congratulated his daughter. "It took me years to learn that one."

"Thank you." Mimi smiled.

Jack followed behind, slouching forward, his hands in his pockets. He looked at his sister with a newfound respect.

"Father! Tell him!" Mimi demanded, walking up to the desk.

"Tell me what?" Jack asked.

Charles Force took a sip from his glass and watched his children with hooded eyes. His so-called children. Madeleine Force and Benjamin Force. Two of the most powerful Blue Bloods of all time. They had been there in Rome, during the crisis. They had founded Plymouth, they had settled the New World. He had been the one to call them up again and again, whenever they were needed.

"About the Van Alen mongrel," Mimi said. "Tell him."

"What about Schuyler? What do you know?" Jack asked.

"More than you, my brother." Mimi said. She took a seat in one of the leather club chairs across from her father's desk. She turned to her brother, flashing her green eyes at his identical ones. "Unlike you, I've accessed my memories. She's not in them. I've checked. Again and again. She's not there. She's not anywhere. She isn't supposed to exist!" Mimi's voice took on a high screech. Her fangs were bared.

Jack took a step backward. "That can't be. I have her in mine. You couldn't be more wrong. Father, what the hell is she talking about?"

Charles took another sip from his glass and cleared his throat. Finally, he said, "Your sister's right."

"But I don't understand . . ." Jack said, slumping down into the other club chair.

"Technically, Schuyler Van Alen is not a Blue Blood." Charles sighed.

"That's impossible," Jack declared.

"She is and she's not," Charles explained. "She is a product of *Caerimonia Osculor*, of a union between a vampire and a human familiar."

"But we can't reproduce—we don't have the capacity. . . ." Jack argued.

"We cannot *reproduce* among ourselves, that is true. We cannot create new life; we merely carry the spirits of those who have passed in a new embryonic form through in vitro fertilization. I believe it is even common among the Red Bloods these days. Our women are implanted with the seed of an immortal consciousness so that it can take on a new physical shell in the Cycle of Expression.

"But since the Red Bloods have the ability to create new life, new spirits, miscegenation between the two is apparently not impossible. Improbable, but not impossible.

However, in all our years, it has never happened before. To conceive a baby of mixed blood is against the strictest laws of our kind. Her mother was a troubled and foolish woman."

Mimi poured some of the liquid in the decanter into a new Baccarat glass. She took a sip. Rothschild Cabernet. "She should have been destroyed," she hissed.

"No!" Jack cried.

"Do not be so alarmed. Nothing is going to happen to her," Charles said soothingly. "The Committee has not come to a definitive conclusion concerning her fate. She appears to have inherited some of her mother's traits, so we have kept close watch on her."

"You're going to kill her, aren't you?" Jack said, his head in his hands. "I won't let you."

"That is not for you to decide. Look deep into your memories, Benjamin. Tell me what you see. Look for the truth inside yourself."

Jack closed his eyes. When they had danced at the Informals, he had felt Schuyler's presence in his own memories as if he had known her from out of time. He went back to that night, to the room where they were dancing at the American Society mansion, and to the memory of the night of the Patrician Ball—the night they had waltzed to Chopin. One of his most vivid and treasured memories—it was . . . her . . . it couldn't be anyone else! There! He felt triumphant! He looked closely at the face behind the fan. There was the fair, porcelain skin, the delicate features, that upturned nose, and he recoiled—those weren't Schuyler's eyes—those eyes were green, not blue—those eyes were . . .

"Her mother's," Jack said, opening his own eyes and looking at his father and sister.

Charles nodded. His voice was uncharacteristically harsh. "Yes. You saw Allegra Van Alen. It's a powerful resemblance. Allegra was one of our best."

Jack lowered his head. He had projected that image onto Schuyler when they were dancing, had used his vampire powers to fill her own senses, so that she thought she had sensed the past as well. But Schuyler was a new soul. Her mother, it was her mother whom Jack had pursued across the centuries. That's why he'd been drawn to Schuyler, ever since that night in front of Block 122—because her face was so like the one that haunted his dreams.

Then he looked up at Mimi. His sister. His partner, his better half, his best friend and worst enemy. It was she who had been with him since the beginning. It was her hand that he reached for now in the darkness. She was strong, she was a survivor. It was from her that he drew his strength. She had always been there for him. Agrippina to his Valerius. Elisabeth de Lorraine-Lillebonne when he was Louis d'Orleans. Susannah Fuller to his William White.

Mimi reached over and took his hand in hers. They were so alike; they had come from the same dark fall, from the same expulsion that had cursed them to live their immortal lives on earth, and yet, here they were, thriving after a millennia. She patted his hand, the tears in her eyes mirroring his own.

"So what do we do now?" Jack asked. "What's going to happen to her?"

"For now, nothing. We watch and wait. It's probably best if you stay clear of her. And your sister has informed me about your concerns about Augusta's death. I'm pleased to say we are very close to finding the perpetrator. I am sorry to have kept you both in the dark for so long. Let me explain. . . ."

Jack nodded and gripped his sister's hand even more tightly.

he next week went by swiftly. Every day after school, Schuyler and Oliver hit the stacks at the Repository, trying to find any record or mention of "Croatan." They combed through the computer database, trying every conceivable spelling of the word. But since the library files were only automated in the late 1980s, they also had to reference the ancient card catalog.

"Can I help you?" a grave voice asked as they huddled together at Oliver's desk one afternoon, poring over dozens of old books and several cards from the "Cr–Cu" drawer.

"Oh, Master Renfield. May I introduce Schuyler Van Alen?" Oliver asked, standing up and making a small, formal bow.

Schuyler shook the old man's hand. He had a haughty, aristocratic visage and was dressed in an anachronistic Edwardian greatcoat and velvet trousers. Oliver had told her about

Renfield—a human Conduit who took his job way too seriously. "He's been serving the Blue Bloods for so long he thinks he *is* a vampire. Classic Stockholm Syndrome," Oliver had said.

"I think we've got it covered." Oliver smiled nervously. They had tacitly decided not to ask any of the librarians for any help with their search, intuitively understanding that it was an illicit subject. If The Committee was hiding something, and that something had to do with "Croatan," then it was probably best if they didn't tell anyone about it.

Renfield picked up a piece of paper from Oliver's desk, where Schuyler had scribbled down a series of words. "Croatan? Kroatan? Chroatan? Chroatin? Kruatan?" He quickly put the paper down, as if it burned his fingers.

"Croatan. I see," he said.

Oliver attempted a casual tone. "It's just something we heard about. It's nothing. Just a school project."

"A school project," Renfield nodded somberly. "Of course. Unfortunately, I have never heard of the word. Would you care to enlighten me?"

"I think it's a piece of cheese. Something to do with an old English recipe." Oliver replied with a straight face. "From Blue Blood banquets in the sixteenth century."

"Cheese. I see."

"Like Roquefort or Camembert. But I'm thinking it's more like a sheep's milk, maybe," Oliver said. "Or a goat. It could be a goat. Or maybe like a mozzarella. What do you think, Sky?"

Schuyler's lips were twitching and she couldn't trust herself to answer.

"Very well. Carry on," Renfield said, leaving them to their task.

When he was safely at a far distance, Schuyler and Oliver burst out laughing—as softly as they could.

"Cheese!" Schuyler whispered. "I thought he was going to faint!"

It was the one bright spot in an otherwise dreary week. The colder weather brought a rash of ailments. The flu bug hit the school, and several students had been out for the past couple of days, Jack Force among them. Apparently, even vampires weren't immune to the flu epidemic. Schuyler also heard Bliss had been grounded since the party, and the tall Texan girl kept to herself. Even Dylan complained about it—Bliss was moody and remote, and never left Mimi's side.

The next day was bitter cold and gray. The first sign that winter was approaching. It was a New York gray—from the buildings to the smog to the skies—as if a dark, damp cloud had descended on the city like a wet blanket. When Schuyler arrived at the Duchesne gates, a dark mist hung over a bustling commotion in front of the school. She passed several white news vans with satellite antennas, and a crew of reporters primping, checking their teeth in handheld mirrors, and grooming before the cameras rolled. There were camera crews with tripods everywhere, as well as newspaper and magazine reporters and photographers—an even bigger mob than on the day of Aggie's funeral.

Several Duchesne students were huddled at the front doors, watching the scene. She found Oliver in the crowd and joined him.

"What's happened?" she asked.

Oliver looked grim. "Something awful. I feel it."

"I feel it too," she agreed. "It's not another death is it?"

"I'm not sure."

They waited at the gates. From the front door of the Duchesne mansion, two burly policemen were escorting a young man between them. A scruffy, disheveled young man wearing a beat-up leather jacket.

"Dylan! Why? What's he done?" Schuyler asked, horrified.

The crowd of reporters and cameramen pressed forward, covering the scene with flashes and a barrage of questions.

"Any comment?"

"Why did you do it?"

"Care to share your feelings with our readers?"

Schuyler felt panicked and distressed. Why were they taking Dylan away? And in such a public fashion? She couldn't believe the school would let them do something like this! She found a wild-eyed Bliss in the crowd.

"Schuyler!" For the moment, Bliss had forgotten she and Schuyler weren't really friends.

Schuyler took Bliss's hands in hers. "Why? What

happened? Why are they taking him away?" she asked.

"They think Dylan killed Aggie!" she said. Bliss was fighting to hold on to her composure, but seeing Oliver's and Schuyler's stricken faces made her break down. She held on to them for support. "I overheard them talking to the headmistress. Aggie didn't die of a drug overdose, she was murdered . . . strangled, and she had Dylan's DNA on her fingertips. . . ."

"No."

"It's got to be a mistake," Bliss said tearfully.

"Bliss, listen to me," Schuyler said, a hard edge to her voice. "He's being set up. Dylan couldn't have killed Aggie. Remember?"

Bliss's eyes focused. She nodded. She knew what Schuyler was saying. "Because . . ."

"Because he's human and a Red Blood can't kill a Blue Blood. . . . Aggie would have overpowered him in a second. It's a lie. Aggie was a vampire. There was no way Dylan could have killed her."

"A setup."

"Right," Schuyler said. The rain was coming down in torrents, and all three of them were getting soaked, but none of them seemed to notice.

Bliss looked fearfully at Oliver. "But Schuyler, there's no such thing as a vampire. . . ." she said lamely.

"Oh. Don't worry about Oliver. He knows. He's okay. He's a Conduit. I'll explain later."

Oliver tried to look trustworthy and reassuring. He remembered his umbrella in his pack and opened it, shielding them from the rain.

"Jack told me last week that there's something out there killing Blue Bloods. My guess is Dylan's being framed," Schuyler explained.

"So that means he's innocent. . . ." Bliss said hopefully.

"Of course he is. We need to find out who is behind this, and we need to get Dylan out of there." Schuyler declared.

Bliss nodded.

"We need to find out what's going on. Why Dylan is being charged all of a sudden, when the official report was a drug overdose. Where did they get this 'evidence'? And why Dylan?"

"Your dad's a senator. He's got to have some connections with the police department. Can't he help?" Oliver suggested.

"I'll ask him," Bliss promised. The three of them walked through the school gates. They were already late for their homeroom classes.

Later, at lunch, Bliss met up with Oliver and Schuyler at the cafeteria. They were seated at the back table as usual, hidden behind the marble fireplace.

"You spoke to your dad?" Schuyler asked.

"What did he say?" Oliver prodded.

Bliss pulled out a chair next to them and planted her elbows on the table. She rubbed her eyes and looked at the two of them. "He said, don't worry about your friend. The Committee is taking care of this."

Schuyler and Oliver digested the information. "That's strange isn't it?" Schuyler asked. "Because Committee meetings have been canceled until further notice."

THIRTY-TWO

The whole school was still buzzing with the news that afternoon—and in Schuyler's ethics class, Mr. Orion was trying to calm down his students.

"Settle down, settle down, please," he said. "I know this is a tough time, but we need to remember that in the United States, we are innocent until proven guilty."

Schuyler walked into the room and noticed that Jack was back in his usual seat next to the window.

"Hey," she said, giving him a shy smile and taking the desk next to his. She would never forget the way he'd kissed her, almost as if he'd kissed her before.

Jack looked more handsome than she'd ever seen him. His hair gleamed white-gold underneath the light, and his clothes were crisply pressed, his shirt neatly tucked for once. He was wearing a black sweater and a gold watch she'd never seen on his wrist before. He didn't look up at her.

"Jack . . ."

"Yes?" he asked coldly.

Schuyler recoiled at the arctic tone in his voice. "Is something wrong?" she whispered.

He didn't reply.

"Jack, we have to do something! They've arrested Dylan! And you know it's wrong. He couldn't have killed her!" She whispered fiercely. "He's human. He's being set up. We need to find out why."

Jack took out his fountain pen and scratched the nib on his notebook. He didn't look at her. "It's none of our business."

Schuyler whispered fiercely, "But what do you mean? You know it is. We need to find out about what's killing us off. Don't you—didn't you want to—?"

"Care to share with the rest of the class, Miss Van Alen?" Mr. Orion asked, interrupting the conversation.

Schuyler slouched down in her seat. "No, sorry."

For the rest of the period, Jack sat silent and stony-faced. He refused to look at Schuyler, or even to read the notes she passed to him.

When the bell rang signaling the end of class, Schuyler ran after him.

"What's gotten into you? Is it your sister? What's wrong?"

Jack snapped. "Don't bring Mimi into this."

"But I don't understand. What you said on Saturday night—"

"I spoke recklessly. It's not the way I feel. I'm sorry to have misled you."

"Why are you shutting me out? What's happened to you?" Schuyler asked, a catch in her voice.

Jack looked Schuyler up and down. "I'm really sorry, Schuyler. But I made a mistake. I shouldn't have said the things I said that night. I was wrong. My father set me straight. The Committee isn't hiding anything. They've investigated the circumstances of Aggie's death, and we just need to trust them to know what's best. They'll let us know once it's been resolved. I think we should just forget about the whole thing."

"Your father—your father has something to do with this, doesn't he?" she accused him.

He put a heavy hand on her shoulder, gripped it tightly, then released it, pushing himself away. "Leave it alone, Schuyler. For your sake and mine."

"Jack!" she called.

He didn't turn around. She saw him walk purposefully down to the second landing, where Mimi Force was coming out of a classroom. She saw the two of them together, noticing as if for the first time that they had the same lithe form, the same panther limbs, they were the same height, the same coloring. She saw Mimi smile when she saw Jack. As Jack slung an arm around his sister's shoulders in an intimate and affectionate way, something in her heart broke.

"What did Jack say?" Bliss asked, meeting Schuyler and

Oliver for coffee at the Starbucks across the street during their free period.

"He's no help," Schuyler said, the words dead in her mouth.

"Why not?"

"He's changed his mind. He says that what he told me was a mistake. He told me to forget about it." She tore a paper napkin into tiny pieces, meticulously ripping it apart until her tray was filled with confetti. "He said The Committee will explain everything in time, we just need to be patient," she said bitterly.

"But what about Dylan?" Bliss asked. "We can't just let them charge him for something he didn't do!"

"We're not. It's up to us," Oliver said. "We're the only ones who can help him now."

THIRTY-THREE

*T*he police wouldn't let them see Dylan. They tried to visit him after school, but they encountered a wall of law enforcement—and no one at the station would even admit to holding him there. It was a dead end. They had taken away his cell phone and his Sidekick, and they had no way to get in touch with him. Schuyler felt a deep sense of foreboding. The crisis brought the three of them—Bliss, Schuyler, and Oliver—closer than ever. The next day, Bliss stopped sitting with Mimi in the cafeteria. Instead, they spent every free period plotting on how to help their friend.

"His family's rich. I'm sure they have some awesome defense lawyer set up for him, right?" Bliss asked. "We need to talk to them. I need to tell them something."

"What?" Schuyler asked.

"I did a little investigating on my own last night. Okay, so I overheard my mom talking to some people about the case.

I heard her say the police said time of death was between ten and eleven P.M. They're pretty sure about that. The way Aggie's body was found, it couldn't have happened anytime earlier or later."

"So?" From a skeptical Oliver.

"So, Dylan was with me from ten to eleven. We were outside in the alley the whole time, smoking cigarettes. He never left my side."

"Not once? Not even to go to the bathroom?" Schuyler asked.

Bliss shook her head. "No. I'm positive. I looked at my watch a couple of times. Because I was, uh, worried, that Mimi would wonder where I was."

"You know what that means, don't you?" Oliver asked. He was smiling.

The two girls shook their heads.

"It means he has a rock-solid alibi. Bliss Llewellyn, you are a doll. You're his get-out-of-jail-free card. C'mon, we've got to find Dylan's family and tell them."

Dylan lived in Tribeca, so they took Bliss's Rolls Royce down to his neighborhood that afternoon. Oliver and Schuyler were impressed by the plush interior. "I've got to get my dad to get us one of these," Oliver marveled. "We only have a boring old Town Car."

Tribeca was a former industrial neighborhood—the old butter and egg district, with cobblestone streets and old factory buildings turned into multimillion-dollar lofts.

"Is this the address?" Oliver asked, walking toward a loft building on the corner. They consulted the Duchesne address book. It was.

"You've never been here?" Bliss asked, surprised.

Oliver and Schuyler shook their heads.

"But I thought you were his friends."

"We are," Schuyler said. "But see . . ."

"It never occurred to us. . . ." Oliver explained.

Schuyler sighed. "We always hung out at Oliver's. He has TiVo and an Xbox. Dylan never seemed to mind."

"What about you? You're like, his girlfriend. You've never been here?" Oliver asked.

Bliss shook her head. She wasn't really his girlfriend. They'd never really defined their relationship. They'd hooked up a couple of times, and she was going to make him her human familiar and everything, but after they'd been caught the night of the party, her parents had forbidden her to see him. Somehow, her parents had got it in their heads that the party had been his idea. BobiAnne still couldn't forgive the fact that the Cinderella mannequin had come back from New Jersey stripped of its ballgown. All was not well at Penthouse des Rêves.

"Hi, we're looking for apartment 1520?" Schuyler asked the doorman as they entered the building. Unlike the grand palatial majesty of the typical Park Avenue co-op, the Tribeca building was modern and sleek, with a Zen garden and a waterfall in the lobby.

"1520?" was the doubtful reply.

"The Ward family?" Bliss added helpfully.

The doorman frowned. "Right. They were in 1520. But the place is up for sale. The family moved out yesterday. Rush job."

"Are you sure?"

"Positive, miss."

The doorman even let them look inside the empty apartment. It was a huge, six thousand square-foot loft, and there was nothing in it but an abandoned television set. The walls were scratched from the furniture, and there was a ghostly outline of an L-shaped couch on the floor.

"It's selling for about five million, if anyone's interested," the doorman added. "I've got the broker's info downstairs."

"This just doesn't make sense." Schuyler said. "Why would his family move out so quickly? Don't they have enough to worry about with Dylan in jail?"

They walked around the empty apartment, as if trying to conjure up a reason for the Wards' sudden disappearance.

"Do you know where they went?" Schuyler asked the helpful doorman.

"Something about going back to Connecticut, I heard. Not sure."

The doorman led them out of the apartment and locked it behind them. They took the elevator back down to the lobby. Bliss took out the Duchesne directory from her Chloé Paddington bag. But the phone numbers for Dylan's parents listed in the book were out of service. There were no new listings.

"Did you guys ever meet his parents?" Bliss asked, putting her cell phone away.

Again, Schuyler and Oliver shook their heads.

"I think he had a brother in college," Schuyler volunteered, feeling more and more guilty for not knowing much about their friend. They hung out at school every day, and every weekend. And yet, when pressed, neither Schuyler nor Oliver could remember anything about Dylan's background.

"He didn't talk about himself much," Oliver said. "He was kind of quiet."

"He probably couldn't get a word in," Bliss joked. "Between the two of you, I mean—when you're together you guys tend to take over."

Schuyler accepted the observation without feeling insulted. They did tend to take over. She and Oliver had been friends for so long, and they were so used to each other, it was a miracle that Dylan had found a way to ingratiate himself into their partnership, making the duo a trio. They had let him, mostly because they were flattered that he liked them so much, but also because he didn't get in the way. He seemed to enjoy their stories, their inside jokes, and never seemed to want more than what they could give him.

"If we could only talk to him," Schuyler said.

"If we could only explain to the police," Oliver added.

"Explain what?" Bliss asked huffily. "That he couldn't

have killed her because she was a vampire and nothing can kill vampires, except for, oh, some weird thing we don't know about yet, but by the way, Dylan's human so . . . well, when you look at it that way, who's ever going to believe us?" Bliss asked.

"Nobody," Schuyler concluded.

They stood in front of Dylan's former apartment building, stymied and frustrated.

THIRTY-FOUR

*S*ince there was nothing they could do for Dylan right then, Oliver suggested visiting the Repository in the basement of The Bank again. On the way, he and Schuyler filled Bliss in on what they knew. They had to keep trying. So far, none of their leads had led to anything, especially since they didn't even know how to spell Croatan.

"What about looking up Plymouth instead?" Oliver suddenly asked. "Sky, you said Jack Force mentioned it was part of his memory that was blocked out. Something about the Plymouth Colony."

The Repository was emptier than usual, and the three of them diligently set about their tasks. Schuyler found several history books documenting the colonization of Plymouth and the *Mayflower* passage, Bliss found an interesting record of every passenger on the *Mayflower*, and Oliver came up with a large, leather-bound book that contained civil documents. But nothing included any mention of Croatan.

"Looking for cheese again?" Renfield asked, gliding past their table.

"Cheese?" Bliss asked, confused, while Oliver and Schuyler chuckled.

"We'll tell you later," Schuyler promised.

A little while later, Bliss and Schuyler remembered they had an appointment with the Stitched for Civilization crew to go over their photographs, so they left Oliver for the rest of the afternoon. The new advertisement was going to be rolled out on a billboard in Times Square the next week, and Jonas wanted to show them the final image they'd chosen.

During the meeting, Schuyler's cell phone rang. "It's Oliver," she told Bliss. "I should get it." She excused herself from the table. "What's up?" she asked.

"Come back, I think I've found something," he said, the excitement palpable in his voice.

When they returned to the Repository, Oliver showed them what he'd found. It was a slim, leather-bound book. "It was hidden so far back in the stacks I almost missed it. It's a diary, by a woman who was one of the original settlers in Plymouth. See what she says. . . ."

They read the pages, documenting the journey across the sea, the foundation of the colony, her husband's trip to Roanoke, and the final, frantic entry. The writing was almost incomprehensible, as if the writer had been almost too frightened to write the words on the page.

But there it was.

CROATAN.

"A single word, written in a message on a tree." Oliver intoned. *"They are here. We are not safe."*

"It's happened before," Schuyler said. "That's what Jack told me. It must have happened then as well. That must be what she is talking about. What they were frightened of."

"You're right. Croatan must mean something—they're scared of it. It has to be the key." Oliver said.

"Croatan," Bliss said, the word rang distant alarm bells in her memory. "I think I've heard of it somewhere." Her brow furrowed. "And she talks about Roanoke. You remember Roanoke, right?"

"I'm not real good at history, actually," Schuyler apologized. "But it had something to do with a missing colony, right?"

"The Lost Colony," Oliver agreed. "I don't know why it didn't occur to me before. It was the original colony, settled several years before Plymouth. But they all disappeared. There was nothing left of the colony."

"Right. They all died, remember? Nobody ever found out what happened to them. It's an unsolved mystery of American history," Bliss added. "Like the JFK assassination."

"They must have been Blue Bloods," Oliver said.

"And they were all killed. At least, Catherine Carver seemed to think so." Schuyler nodded.

"Is that all there is?" Schuyler asked.

"There's just one more page," Oliver said, showing them the last page of the diary. "About some kind of election or something. Here she writes, 'Flee or stay?' Well, we know what happened. They stayed. The Blue Bloods stayed. We wouldn't be here if they hadn't. Myles Standish—whoever he is, he must have won."

"There's nothing more about Croatan, or Roanoke, or anything?" Bliss asked, taking the diary and flipping the pages.

"No. That's it. The diary just ends. Like the pages have been torn out and someone doesn't want us to know about it, or something. But I did find something. Look here, there's a list of the last people who've borrowed it."

They looked to where he was pointing. There was a yellow flap listing the names of the Blue Bloods who had borrowed the diary.

"Most of them are so old, they're gone by now. But look at the final one."

Schuyler peered at the borrower list. The final signature contained three letters written delicately in fine script. CVA. 12/24/11.

"Whoever borrowed this did so in 1911, and that means, they're—"

"Over a hundred years old by now," Bliss interrupted. "How do we know they're still in this cycle?"

"It's possible. Anyway, it's the only chance we've got," Oliver said.

"CVA?" Bliss asked. "Who's CVA?"

"CVA," Schuyler repeated. The letters were familiar, as was the spidery writing. "Those are my grandmother's initials. CVA. Cordelia Van Alen. And it looks like her handwriting. I'm sure of it."

"You think she borrowed this book? Maybe she knows something about it?" Bliss asked.

Schuyler shrugged. "I don't know, but I could ask her."

"When is she getting back from Nantucket?" Oliver asked.

"Tomorrow. I'm supposed to meet her at the Conservatory lunch. I almost forgot," Schuyler said.

"So, Oliver, this Croatan thing, that's what's behind Aggie's death?" Bliss asked.

"I think so," Oliver said. "Although I still don't know what it *is*."

"But even if we did find out, it still doesn't do anything for Dylan. Even if Croatan is what killed Aggie, how are we going to prove Dylan didn't do it? How are we going to prove he's been set up?" Bliss asked.

"We don't," Oliver said. "I mean, you guys don't. I don't know how much help I can be."

"What do you mean? You've already done so much," Schuyler protested. She gave him an admiring glance that made him blush.

"Research, yes. I can do research. That's what we're good for, but I can't do anything to help with the plan."

"What plan?" Bliss asked, amused.

Oliver looked so serious and purposeful for a second. He had dropped his glib jokes for once. "We've been acting as if the system works for us. It doesn't. You need to think like Blue Bloods. We're never going to convince anyone to let Dylan out based on what we know. So we do something else," Oliver said.

"What?"

"Bust him out."

he Central Park Conservatory luncheon was one of the most important events on Cordelia's social calendar. It was held in a ballroom at the Plaza, and was already well under way when Schuyler arrived. She checked in at the registration table and found her grandmother seated in the center with well-preserved luminaries on either side.

"My granddaughter, Schuyler," Cordelia said, looking pleased.

Schuyler pecked her grandmother's cheek. She took a seat at the table, removing a program from her chair.

The yearly luncheon raised a significant sum for the upkeep and maintenance of the park. It was one of the Blue Bloods most cherished causes. It had been their idea to bring nature to New York, to bring an oasis to the heart of the city, a simulacrum of the Garden they had been banished from so long ago. Schuyler recognized many of the grande dames and socialites from The Committee meetings flitting about from table to table, greeting guests.

"Cordelia—what's Croatan?" Schuyler demanded, breaking in to the gossipy chitchat.

The table went silent, and several ladies raised their eyebrows at Schuyler and her grandmother.

Cordelia startled at the word. She broke the roll she was holding in two. "This is neither the time nor the place, young lady," she said quietly.

"I know you know. We saw it in one of the Repository books. It had your initials in them. Cordelia, I have to know." Schuyler whispered fiercely.

At the podium, the mayor was thanking the ladies of the conversancy for their generous donations and efforts to keep Central Park a vibrant and beautiful place. There was a ripple of applause, under which Cordelia admonished her granddaughter.

"Not now. I will tell you afterward, but you will not embarrass me at this function."

For the next hour, Schuyler sat glumly, picking at the herb chicken on her plate and listening to a host of speakers describe the new activities and developments planned for the park. There was a slide show on the new art exhibit, and a presentation on the restoration of Bethesda Fountain.

Finally, after they were given their gift bags, and she and Cordelia were safely ensconced in Cordelia's ancient limousine, with Julius driving, did Schuyler get her answers.

* * *

"So you've found Catherine's diary. Yes, I left my initials there. For someone to find. I didn't know it would be you," Cordelia said, amused.

"It wasn't me. It was Oliver Hazard-Perry actually."

"Ah. Oliver, yes. A very helpful boy. From an excellent family. For Red Bloods, that is."

"Don't change the subject. What's Croatan?"

Cordelia raised the partition separating them from Julius. When it was fully closed, she turned to Schuyler with a frown. "What I am going to tell you is verboten. We cannot speak of it. The Committee has legislated it out of existence. They have even tried to suppress it from our memories."

"Why?" Schuyler asked, looking out the window at the city. It was another gray day, and Manhattan seemed to be lost in a fine mist, ghostly and majestic.

"As I told you, times have changed. The old ways are no more. The people in power do not believe. Even the woman who wrote that diary would disown her words. It would be too dangerous for her to admit her fears."

"How do you know she would feel that way?" Schuyler asked.

"Simple, because I wrote it. It's my diary."

"You're Catherine Carver?" Schuyler asked.

"Yes. I remember the Plymouth settlement clearly, almost as if it were yesterday. It was a terrible journey." She shuddered. "And an even more terrible winter followed it."

250

"Why? What happened?

"Croatan." Cordelia sighed. "An ancient word. It means Silver Blood."

"Silver Blood?"

"You were told the story of our Expulsion."

"Yes." The car slowly made its way across Fifth Avenue. Because of the bad weather, there were only a few people milling outside the department stores, a handful of tourists taking pictures of the window dressing, shoppers trying to get out of the rain.

"When God cast out Lucifer and his angels from heaven, as punishment for their sins, we were cursed to live our immortal lives on Earth, where we became vampires, dependent on human blood to survive," Cordelia said.

"They told us all this at The Committee meetings."

"But they don't tell you this part. It's been stricken from our official records."

"Why?"

Cordelia didn't answer. Instead, her voice took on a monotone quality, as if she were reading from a book committed to memory. "Early in our history, Lucifer and a small host of his loyal followers broke off from the group. They rejected God, and were contemptuous of their banishment. They did not want to regain the Lord's Grace. They did not believe in the Code of the Vampires."

"Why not?" Schuyler asked, as the car idled at the light. They were on Sixth Avenue now, among the skyscrapers and corporate office buildings with the names of their companies engraved on the façade. McGraw-Hill. Simon and Schuster. Time Warner. A bank of televisions in the Morgan Stanley building blasted the latest news from the stock market.

"Because they did not want to live within any kind of law. They were willful and arrogant, on earth as they were in heaven. Lucifer and his vampires discovered that performing *Caerimonia Osculor* on other vampires instead of humans made them more powerful. As you know, *Caerimonia Osculor* is the sucking of blood that vampires commit on humans in order to gain strength. In the Code of the Vampires, it is forbidden to perform the *Caerimonia Osculor* on fellow Blue Bloods. But this is exactly what Lucifer and his vampires did. They began to consume Blue Bloods to complete Dissipation."

"You mean—"

"Until they had sucked out the very life force from a being, yes. Until they had consumed a Blue Blood and all his memories."

"But why? And what happened then?"

"By consuming the Blue Blood's life force, Lucifer and his vampires' blood turned Silver. They become the Silver Bloods. *Croatan*. It means Abomination. They are insane, with the lives of many vampires in their heads. They have the strength of a thousand Blue Bloods. Their memories are legion. They are the devil in disguise, the devil that walks among us; they are everywhere and nowhere."

As Cordelia spoke, they drove past Sixth Avenue to

Seventh, and the neighborhood changed again. Schuyler saw Carnegie Hall on the corner and several people lined up outside buying tickets, huddled under their umbrellas.

"For thousands of years, the Silver Bloods hunted and killed and consumed Blue Bloods. They broke the Code of the Vampires by directly interfering in human affairs and acquiring power in the world of men. They were unstoppable. But the Blue Bloods never stopped fighting them. It was the only way to survive."

"The Last Great War between the Blue Bloods and the Red Bloods ended during the final years of the Roman Empire, when the Blue Bloods were able to unseat Caligula, a powerful and wily Silver Blood vampire. After Caligula was defeated, for many centuries Blue Bloods lived in peace in Europe."

"So why did we come to America?" Schuyler asked, as the car shot up Eighth Avenue.

"Because we were distressed by the religious persecution we found rising in the seventeenth century. So in 1620, we came to the New World on the *Mayflower* with the Puritans, in order to find peace in the New World."

"But there was no peace, was there?" Schuyler said, thinking of Catherine's diary.

"No. There was not," Cordelia said, closing her eyes. "We discovered that Roanoke had been savaged. Everyone was lost. The Silver Bloods were in the New World as well. But that was not the worst."

"Why?"

"Because the killings began again. In Plymouth. Many of our young—Blue Bloods can only be taken during the Sunset Years, when we turn from human to our real vampire selves. It is our most vulnerable time. While we are not in command of our memories, we do not know our strength. We are weak and can be manipulated and controlled, and in the end, consumed by the Silver Bloods."

They drove up the West Side Highway, past the shiny new developments by the river and next to Riverside Park.

"Some refused to believe that the Silver Bloods were responsible. They refused to see what was right in front of them, insisting that those who had been consumed would be able to return somehow. They were blind to the threat. And after a few years, the killings stopped. The years passed and nothing happened. Then centuries—still nothing. Silver Bloods became a myth, a legend, passing into a quaint fairy tale. Blue Bloods gained wealth, prominence, and status in America, and as time went on, most of us forgot about the Silver Bloods completely."

"But how? How could we forget something so important?"

Cordelia sighed. "We have become complacent and stubborn. Denial is a strong temptation as well. Now everything about the Silver Bloods has even been removed from our history books. Blue Bloods today refuse to believe that there is anything stronger than them in the world. Their vanity does not allow them to conceive of it."

Schuyler shook her head, appalled.

"Those of us who warned and campaigned for eternal vigilance were banished from The Conclave, and have no power in The Committee today. No one listens to us anymore. No one has listened to us since Plymouth. I tried then, but I was not powerful enough to take control."

"John wanted to raise the alarm," Schuyler said, remembering what the diary had said. "Your husband."

"Yes. But we were unsuccessful. Myles Standish—you know him today as Charles Force—became the head of the Conclave of Elders. He has led us ever since. He does not believe in the danger of Croatan."

"Not even when it kills children?"

"According to Charles, it has not been proven."

"But Jack said all of Aggie's blood was drained, as were two others they'd found earlier. They had to have been consumed by a Silver Blood!"

Cordelia looked grim. "Yes, that is my guess as well. But no one listens to an old woman who has lost her fortune. I never believed the Silver Bloods had gone away entirely. I always thought they were only resting, watching, and waiting, for their time to return."

"That has to be it. That's the only explanation!" Schuyler argued. "But the police arrested my friend Dylan. He couldn't have done it! Dylan's human. They took him away yesterday."

Cordelia looked troubled. "I thought the official

explanation was a drug overdose. I heard that is what The Committee had decided."

"That's what we heard—but now they're saying she was strangled."

"It's true in a sense," Cordelia mused.

"You need to help us. How do we find out who the Silver Bloods are! Why they are here? Where are they? How can we find them?"

"Something has awakened them. Something is harboring them. They could be anyone we know. Silver Bloods disguised as Blue Bloods in our midst. It takes a long time to turn a Blue Blood into a Silver Blood. My guess is that a powerful Silver Blood has returned, and is beginning to recruit new disciples."

"So what do we do now?" Schuyler asked, as the car pulled up to their street.

"You have the knowledge of the Silver Bloods. You at least know what is out there. You can prepare yourself."

"How?"

"There is one thing. One thing your mother discovered. Silver Bloods are still bound to the laws of heaven and the Sacred Language." She whispered the rest in Schuyler's ear.

Cordelia opened the car door and stepped out. "I can say no more on this matter. I have already broken The Code to tell you this story. As for the problem you have presented, I do apologize, but you are going to have to speak to Charles Force. He is the only one who can help your friend now."

THIRTY-SIX

*T*he Committee meetings were reinstated on Monday. They had been canceled for several weeks, without any explanation given to the junior members. During the meeting, planning for the Four Hundred Ball began in earnest. There was still no mention of Aggie's death or Dylan's arrest. Instead, there was excited chatter for the Christmas formal. The Four Hundred Ball was the most anticipated party of the year, the most glamorous, the most fantastic, and the most exclusive, as only Blue Bloods were invited.

Schuyler went to the meeting just to see if she could still talk some sense into Jack, who was standing with his back to her. The junior members were divided into subcommittees, and Schuyler joined the Invitation group only because it sounded like the least work. Just as she'd thought, the only task they had was to put together the guest list, which would be vetted by the Senior Committee, and then they would stamp and mail the invitations, which were already chosen, designed, and printed.

"I'm worried about Dylan," Bliss said, when the meeting was over. "Where is he? The police still won't say. And my dad keeps telling me to keep out of it."

"I know, I am too." Schuyler nodded, as her gaze drifted over to where Jack was chatting with Mrs. Dupont and Mimi.

"It's a lost cause, Schuyler. I know the Force twins. They stick together."

"I just have to try," Schuyler said wistfully. She still couldn't believe that the boy who'd kissed her so passionately not so long ago was now ignoring her and acting as if nothing had ever happened between them. She couldn't reconcile the Jack who'd told her about his dreams and his blocked memories with the one who was cheerfully debating swing orchestras or jazz bands for the upcoming ball.

"Suit yourself," Bliss sighed. "But don't say I didn't warn you."

Schuyler nodded. Bliss walked away and Schuyler moved toward Jack Force. Thankfully, Mimi had already left the room.

"Jack, you have to listen to me," she said, pulling him aside. "Please."

"Why?"

"I know what The Committee's hiding. I know what Croatan is."

He stopped, gaping at her. "How?" He had avoided meeting her gaze, but he looked at her now—Schuyler's cheeks were blazing red from anger, and she looked even more beautiful than he remembered.

"My grandmother told me." She relayed everything her grandmother had told her about the Silver Bloods, and the killings in Roanoke and Plymouth.

His forehead furrowed. "She isn't allowed to do that. It's privileged information."

"You know about this?"

"I did some research of my own, and my father told me the rest. But it's a dead end."

"What do you mean? It's the first clue."

He shook his head. "Schuyler, I'm sorry to have misled you. But Aggie's death is being taken care of. You have to trust The Committee to do the right thing. Your grandmother told you an old myth. There is no such thing as the Silver Bloods. No one has ever even proved they really existed."

"I don't believe you. We need to convince The Committee to warn everyone. If you don't join me, I'll do it myself."

"There's nothing I can do to stop you?" Jack asked.

Schuyler jutted her chin out in determination. "No." She looked askance at him. Just a few weeks ago, she'd been falling in love with him, with his courage and his bravery. Where was the boy who refused to swallow the lies The Committee told them? Where had he gone? When they had danced together at the Informals, she thought she had never been happier in her life. But Jack wasn't the boy she thought he was. Maybe he never had been.

THIRTY-SEVEN

After the meeting, Schuyler told Bliss and Oliver everything her grandmother had told her about the Silver Bloods, and how Charles Force was the only person who could help them with Dylan's situation. They decided that the next day Schuyler and Bliss would sneak out of their third period class to confront him. Oliver would make some excuse to their art teacher as to why the girls were absent.

They ambushed Mr. Force in front of the Four Seasons restaurant, where he was known to lunch daily. The Four Seasons was located in the Seagram Building on Park Avenue, and from noon to two P.M., it was the center of the Manhattan universe. Media magnates, financial tycoons, publishers, celebrated authors, and personalities made it their personal commissary.

"There he is," Bliss said, spotting his sleek silver head emerging from a black Town Car. She recognized him because her father had hosted the Forces at their apartment the first week they arrived in Manhattan. She had been a bit afraid of Charles Force. The man had looked right through her, as if he knew everything about her, every secret wish, every hidden desire; his handshake had been firm and had left a mark on her. He frightened her, but she wasn't about to let that stop her from helping Dylan.

Schuyler studied him. She could swear she'd seen him before. But where? There was something familiar about him. The way he bent his head forward. She knew this man, she was sure of it.

"Mr. Force! Mr. Force!" Bliss called. Charles Force looked curiously at the two girls standing in front of him.

"Excuse me," he told his lunch partner.

"Mr. Force, we're sorry to disturb you," Bliss said. "But we were told to come to you, that you alone can help us."

"You're Forsyth's kid, right?" Charles said abruptly. "What are you doing here in the middle of the day? Doesn't Duchesne have off-campus rules? Or did that go out with the uniforms?" He turned to Schuyler. "And you." He didn't say her name, but he raised his eyebrows. "If I'm not mistaken you're a Duchesne student as well. Well, you have my attention. How can I help you?"

Schuyler held his gaze and didn't flinch. She stared at him with her bright blue eyes, and it was he who turned away first. "Our friend Dylan is being accused of a murder he didn't commit. You are the only one who can help us. You are the Regis. My grandmother said—"

"Cordelia Van Alen is a menace. She has never forgiven me for taking command of the Conclave," he muttered. He motioned to his lunch partner, who was still patiently holding the door open to the restaurant. "Go ahead, I'll join you in a minute."

"We're not leaving until you help us," Bliss said—her voice quavering—even though there was nothing she wanted more than to run and hide from the man. The voices in her head were screaming, demanding that she stay away from him. *Killer* . . . a voice in her head whispered. *Murderer* . . . She felt a deep and intense revulsion. She wanted to throw up. She wanted to throw herself in front of a cab. She wanted to fly, to flee, anything to escape from his penetrating gaze. She thought she was going to go mad with fright. There was something terrible about this man, a wild and dangerous power she should run from.

"Dylan Ward has been taken care of. There's no need to worry about him anymore," he said, with a dismissive wave of his hand. "He is perfectly safe. Nothing will happen to him. The police made a regrettable mistake. He's free. Your father could have told you that," he sniffed. "He helped with the paperwork for the release."

Bliss was momentarily shocked into silence. She hadn't realized it would be so easy. "What do you mean?"

"Exactly what I said, the matter has been resolved," he

said shortly. "There's no need to worry, I assure you. Now, please, I am late for my lunch."

Bliss and Schuyler exchanged uneasy looks.

"But what about the Silver Bloods? What about what they're doing to us? We know about Croatan!" Schuyler accused.

"Please, don't bother me with Cordelia Van Alen's pitiful fairy tales. I refuse to even discuss it. I've said it before and I'll say it again. There is no such thing as Croatan," he said, a finality to his tone. "Now, I suggest you girls go back to school, where you belong."

he Carlyle Hotel was an understated, elegant hotel on Madison Avenue in the style of a grand English manor. It was one of those hotels that whispered luxury with an intimidating Old Money sang-froid. Even the air-conditioning was always a frosty sixty-six degrees. When Schuyler was little, her grandmother would to take her to the Bemelmans Bar for Shirley Temples. Cordelia would sit at the bar and smoke, drinking one Sazerac after another, and Schuyler would sit quietly, looking at the frolicking animals on the mural and counting the many ladies who came in wearing hats and corsages. Then, afterward, they would repair to the main dining room to tuck into a five-course French meal. On the days when Cordelia declared she'd had "just enough" of the Riverside Drive house, they would repair to a two-bedroom apartment suite at the Carlyle for the weekend. Schuyler would order strawberries and cream from room service, fill up the whirlpool bath, and eat her nutritiously deficient dinner amid the bubbles.

When Schuyler walked into the white marble lobby that evening, she felt at home in the hushed surroundings. She put painful thoughts of Jack Force and the humiliating encounter with his father out of her mind. Bliss had asked her and Oliver to meet her there that evening without explaining why. Oliver was already waiting in a secluded corner of the bar.

"Manhattan?" he asked, motioning to his drink.

"Sure." She nodded.

A discreet waiter arrived bearing a silver tray and her cocktail. He placed a silver bowl of warm Spanish almonds on their table.

Schuyler picked one and munched on it thoughtfully. "God, do they have the best nuts here or what?"

"There's nothing like an Upper East Side hotel." Oliver nodded sagely, taking a handful. "We should do a New York hotel bar-nut tour. Compare the Regency's nuts to the Carlyle's to the St. Regis."

"Mmmmm . . . the Regency has a great selection. They do this little appetizer thing, with three different kinds of treats—wasabi peas, warm nuts, and some kind of peppery cracker," Schuyler said. The Regency was another of Cordelia's favorite haunts.

They emptied their glasses and ordered another. After a few minutes, Bliss ran into the bar, her hair still wet from a shower. She took a seat next to Schuyler and across from Oliver. "Hey, guys. Thanks for meeting me."

"Manhattan?"

"Sure."

The three of them clinked drinks.

"Mmm . . . these nuts are good," Bliss said, popping a few into her mouth.

Oliver and Schuyler laughed.

"What's so funny?"

"Nothing. I'll tell you later, it's not important," Schuyler said.

Bliss raised an eyebrow. The two of them were like that all the time. Inside jokes, memories of their friendship she didn't share. It was amazing that Dylan had put up with it.

"C'mon, what's happened? Why did you want to meet here?" Schuyler asked.

"He's here."

"Who?" Oliver asked.

"Who else? Dylan." Bliss replied. She told them what she found out from her father—that Dylan had been released— but he wasn't exactly as free as Charles Force had told them. Instead, he had been put into protective custody in a suite at the Carlyle Hotel. The judge had allowed Charles Force to bail him out, on the condition that Dylan be released only to his care. Her father said it was all a misunderstanding, and the charges would be dropped soon enough. But they still couldn't figure out why Dylan was being held anyway, especially by Charles Force.

"And I overheard my dad and Charles talking, about how 'they take care of their own' and 'not to let the situation get out of hand.'"

"Wonder what he meant by that?" Schuyler asked, taking another almond from the bowl.

Bliss took a long swig from her cocktail. "Anyway, the way I see it, we just do what Oliver said. Bust him out. We can't fail. Use mind control to overwhelm the guards—Schuyler told me she had done it before—then speed him out of there, and Ollie's the lookout. They're holding him in Room 1001."

"Just like that?" Oliver asked.

"Yeah, why not? You're the one who told us to think like Blue Bloods."

"But how do we get upstairs in the first place? Don't you need to be a guest?" Oliver asked.

"Actually," Schuyler piped up, "that's the easiest part. Cordelia and I used to stay here all the time. I know the elevator guys."

"Well then, let's get the show on the road," Oliver said, raising his hand for the check.

They walked out to the main lobby toward the guarded elevator. "Hey, Marty," Schuyler said, smiling at the elevator man in his shiny red coat with brass buttons.

"Hi, Miss Schuyler, you haven't been here in a while," he said, tipping his hat.

"I know, it's been too long," Schuyler said smoothly, ushering in her friends into the mirrored elevator.

"Twelfth floor?" Marty asked genially.

"No, they uh, put us on ten this time. You guys must be booked."

"It's October," he explained. "Lots of tourists. Some show at the Met or something." He pressed the TEN and took a step back, smiling at Schuyler and her friends.

"Thanks, Marty, see you around!" Schuyler said, when the doors opened.

They walked toward the end of the hallway to the room, but when they arrived at Room 1001, there were no guards stationed at the front of the room.

"That's weird," Bliss said. "I heard my dad saying they've got like, all these cops around him all the time."

Schuyler was about to pulverize the lock, when she noticed something. The door was ajar. She pushed it open. She glanced over her shoulder to find Bliss and Oliver giving her puzzled looks. They had come prepared for battle, and yet there was no obstacle to their progress.

Schuyler entered the room, Bliss immediately behind her.

"Dylan?" Bliss called.

They entered the plush, carpeted room, where the television was still blaring. There was a room service tray with remnants of a steak dinner on its plate, the silver covers haphazardly stacked to the side. An unmade bed and towels on the floor.

"Are you sure they said 1001?" Schuyler asked.

"Completely." Bliss nodded.

"What do you think happened?" Oliver asked, looking around and taking the remote control. He switched off the television.

"Dylan's gone," Bliss said flatly. She remembered what Charles Force had told her. He was being taken care of—whatever that meant. She felt a chill. Had they arrived too late to save him?

"He's escaped." Oliver nodded.

"Or someone, or something, let him go." Schuyler said.

Bliss was silent, her face inscrutable as she looked at the half-eaten meal.

Schuyler placed a sympathetic hand on her shoulder. "I'm sure wherever he is, he's all right. Dylan's tough," she told her friend. "Now, come on, let's get out of here before someone thinks *we* let him out."

THIRTY-NINE

*I*t came upon her without warning. Schuyler cursed her pride. It was all her fault. Oliver had offered to put her in a cab, but since she already owed him so much money, she had declined. Conduit or not, she didn't want to keep taking advantage of his generosity. He and Bliss lived a few blocks away from the Carlyle and she told them she was fine with taking the crosstown bus. The M72 dropped her off at 72nd and Broadway, and she decided to walk the rest of the way home. It was more than twenty blocks, but she looked forward to the exercise.

At the corner of Ninety-fifth Street, she turned from the well-lit avenue to a dark street, hoping to walk up Riverside, and that's when she felt it.

Within seconds, it had her in her grasp. She felt the sharp fangs puncture her skin and begin to slowly draw her life's blood from her. She swooned, gasping. She was going to die.

She was fifteen years old and had hardly even lived, and already she was going to die. She struggled against its iron grip. Worse, knowing what her grandmother had told her, she *would* live. She would live in this foul beast's memory, a trapped prisoner to its insane consciousness forever.

Beauty. Where was Beauty? The bloodhound would be too late to save her now.

The pain was deep; she was feeling dizzy from the blood loss. But just before she succumbed, there was a shout.

A struggle.

Someone was fighting the beast. The Silver Blood was releasing her. She turned, holding her neck to stop the blood flow, to see who had saved her.

Jack Force was trapped in a power struggle with the fell creature, locked in a tremendous fight. It was hulking and large, with shining silver hair and a man's form. But Jack was fighting it.

He matched the Silver Blood blow for blow, but at last, the Silver Blood threw him off, slamming Jack's body against the concrete.

"Jack!" Schuyler screamed. She looked up, and as the monster lunged for her throat, Schuyler remembered her grandmother's words. The laws of heaven meant that any creature was a slave to the Sacred Language.

She held it back with a powerful command: "*Aperio Oris!*" Reveal yourself!

The Silver Blood cackled in laughter, and hissed in a

terrible voice that rasped with the agony of a thousand screaming souls, "You cannot command me, earthspawn!"

The creature continued its menacing march toward her.

"Aperio Oris!" Schuyler shouted again, more forcefully this time.

Jack staggered backward, for in the moment that Schuyler had summoned the incantation, the sacred words that she had learned, the monster had shown them his real face.

It was a face that Jack would never forget.

The beast howled in dismay, screeching a wretched, terrible scream, then disappeared into the night.

"Are you all right?" Schuyler asked, rushing to his side. "You're bleeding."

"It's just a cut," he said, wiping the blood, which had run red, but was blue in the light. "I'm okay. Are you?"

She felt the side of her neck. The bleeding had stopped. "How did you know?" she asked.

"That it would attack you? Because it had once before, so I knew it would do it again. Killers tend to go back and finish what they started."

"But why—"

"I didn't want to see you get hurt because of me," Jack explained brusquely.

Is that all? Schuyler wondered.

"Thank you," she said softly.

"Did you see it?" Jack asked. "Did you?"

"Yes." She nodded. "I did."

"It can't be right," Jack said. "It's a trick." He shook his head. "I don't believe it."

"It's not. It has to follow the laws." Schuyler said gently.

"I know about the Sacred Language," Jack snapped. "But it has to be a mistake."

"No mistake. Those are the rules of creation."

Jack glowered. "No."

The monster had shown itself for one brief moment, when it had no choice but to obey Schuyler's words. The monster had shown its true form. And it was the face of the authority behind New York, the face of the man who single-handedly changed the city to bend to his will.

The face of Charles Force.

His own father.

chuyler told Jack everything she'd put together, hoping that it wasn't true. "It's him. He was there on the night Aggie died. I saw him at the basement of The Bank. He was coming out of the Repository. I remember now. It puts him in the scene of the crime. It was him, Jack."

Jack shook his head.

"You can't deny what you saw. It was your father's face."

"You're wrong. It's a trick of the light, something else." He kept shaking his head and staring down at the blood on the sidewalk.

"Listen to me. Jack, we have to find him. My grandmother said Silver Bloods don't even know what they are. Your father might not even realize he's been possessed."

Jack didn't argue this time.

She put a hand on his arm. "Where is he?"

"Where he always is. The hospital."

"What do you mean? What hospital?"

"Columbia Pres, but I don't know what room. I don't know what he does up there. Only that he visits someone there a lot." Jack said. "Why?"

"I think I might know where we can find him," Schuyler said.

Schuyler felt dire trepidation as they shared a taxicab up to hospital, but she tried to suppress it. When they arrived at the complex, the guards joked about her "boyfriend" as they gave Jack a visitor's tag.

"Who's here? Where are we going?" he asked, as he followed her swiftly down the hallway.

"My mother," Schuyler said. "You'll see."

"Your mother? I thought your mother was dead."

"She might as well be," Schuyler said grimly.

She led him down the empty hallways to the corner room. She looked through the glass window and motioned for Jack to do the same.

There was a man there, kneeling at the foot of the bed. The same mysterious visitor who came every Sunday, whom Schuyler had seen more than once in her mother's room. So that was why Charles Force had looked so familiar to her at Aggie's funeral. Now she recognized the set of the shoulders. He was the man in the basement of The Bank, and the beast who had just attacked her. The dark stranger wasn't her father after all, but a Silver Blood. A monster. She felt a furious rage—what if Charles Force had had something to do with her mother's condition? *What had he done to her?*

"Father," Jack said as he entered the room. He stopped and stared when he saw the face of the woman in the bed. The woman in his dreams. Allegra Van Alen.

Charles looked up and saw Schuyler and Jack standing in front of him. "I thought we had put an end to this," he said, frowning at the two of them together.

"Where were you half an hour ago?" Schuyler demanded.

"Here."

"Liar," Schuyler accused. "CROATAN!"

Charles raised his eyebrows. "Should I be insulted? Please lower your voice. Show some respect for your surroundings. We're in a hospital, not at a wrestling match."

"It's you, Father. We saw you." Jack said. He still couldn't believe Allegra was still alive. But what was she doing in a hospital?

"What exactly are you both accusing me of?"

"Where did you get those scratches?" Jack demanded, noticing the cuts on his father's face.

"Your mother's confounded Persian," Charles growled.

"I don't think so," Schuyler scoffed.

"What is this all about?" Charles demanded. "Why are the two of you here?"

"You attacked Schuyler. I held you off. It was you, I saw you. . . . Schuyler said the words, and my foe revealed its face. And it was yours."

"Is this what you believe?"

"Yes."

"Your grandmother is right, Schuyler," Charles said in a bemused tone. "Times have certainly changed if my own son thinks I am Abomination. That is what you're calling me, isn't it, Jack?" he asked, as he pulled down his shirt cuff and showed them a mark on the underhand of his right wrist. It was of a sword, a golden sword piercing a cloud.

"What is it? Why are you showing us this?" Schuyler asked.

"The mark of the Archangel," Jack explained, his voice reverent. He forgot about his confusion concerning Allegra Van Alen for a moment, and dropped to his knees, prostrating himself in front of his father's feet.

"Precisely," Charles said with a thin smile.

"What does it mean?" Schuyler asked.

"It means, my father is no more a Silver Blood than you or I," Jack explained, his voice rising. "The mark of the Archangel. It can't be duplicated and it can't be falsified. My father is Michael, Pure of Heart, who voluntarily accompanied the banished onto the earth to guide us in our immortal journey." He bowed to his father. "Forgive me. I have been lost, but now I am found."

"Rise, my son. There is nothing to forgive."

Schuyler looked from father to son with questioning eyes. "But I used the Sacred Language. The incantation to reveal its true nature."

"Silver Bloods are agile shape-shifters," Charles

explained. "It would follow your command—but only after showing you something it knew would throw you off, to shock you. Only afterward would it show its true identity. But only for the briefest moment."

"So if your father isn't the Silver Blood, then who is?" Schuyler asked suspiciously. "And where's Dylan?"

"He's safe. For now. Hidden. He won't harm anyone else anymore," Charles said. "Tomorrow he will be far away."

"What do you mean, *harm anyone?*" Schuyler asked.

"He had the bites on his neck. He was being used. Turned."

"Into what? What are you talking about?"

"Dylan's a Blue Blood," Charles said shortly. "At least, he was. I thought you knew that."

Schuyler shook her head. Dylan was a vampire? But then that meant—that meant he could have killed Aggie— that meant that everything they thought, everything they assumed could no longer be true. Dylan wasn't human. Which meant there was a chance he wasn't innocent.

"But he was never at any meetings," Schuyler said weakly.

Charles smiled. "They are not mandatory. You can learn about your history or choose to ignore it. Dylan chose to ignore it. To his detriment. The Silver Bloods only attack the weak-minded. They are drawn to those that are broken, damaged somehow. They sensed Dylan's weakness and preyed on it. Dylan, in turn, preyed on others."

"So then it *was* him. *He* killed Aggie?"

"It is unfortunate what happened with Aggie, yes. We have discovered that Dylan had been drained of almost all his blood in the original attack, but the Silver Blood decided not to consume him totally and turned him into one of them instead. To survive, he had to take a victim of his own," Charles explained. "I am sorry."

Schuyler was speechless for a moment. All along, all along they had thought he was their friend. Dylan, a vampire . . . worse, a Silver Blood's pawn. It was horrifying. "So, Silver Bloods do exist. You admit that they have returned."

"I admit nothing," Charles declared haughtily. "There could be other explanations for his actions. Dylan could still be acting on his own. It does happen once in a while. Dementia. The Sunset Years are volatile ones for our kind. He could have faked the marks on his neck. We must investigate through the proper channels. If he has been corrupted, there is still a chance to save his soul. For now we have placed him and his parents in a safe location."

"But you can't do this. Cover it up. You must warn everybody. You must."

"Just like your grandmother, you are," Charles said. "A pity. Your mother was not a hysterical woman." He looked tenderly down at Allegra and lowered his voice. "The Conclave will take care of it. We will act in time."

"Yet in Plymouth, you did nothing," Schuyler accused. "Roanoke—they were all taken, yet you did nothing."

"And the deaths stopped," Charles said coldly. "If we

had frightened everyone, if we had continued to run, as your grandparents advised, we would never be where we are now. We would be hiding forever, afraid of a shadow that may not exist."

"But Aggie—and the girl from Connecticut and the Choate boy," Schuyler argued. "What about them?"

Charles sighed. "Unfortunate losses, all of them, yes."

Schuyler couldn't believe what she was hearing. Talking about people as if their lives were expendable.

"We will clear this all up in time, I assure you," Charles said. "We won the battle in Rome. The Silver Bloods are all but destroyed."

"My grandmother said that one of them lived, that one of them was able to hide among us . . . that the most power-ful Silver Blood may still be alive," Schuyler said, walking around her mother's bed to face Charles head-on.

"Cordelia has always said that. She persists in saying that. She is mistaken. I was there. I was there at the battle at the temple. Listen to me closely, both of you, because I do not want to repeat this again—I sent Lucifer himself to the fires of hell," Charles declared.

Schuyler was subdued and silent.

"Now, let us leave your mother in peace," Charles ordered. He knelt down again and kissed Allegra's cold hand.

"But there is one thing," Schuyler suddenly remem-bered. "Dylan."

"Yes?" Charles asked.

"Where is he?"

"At the Carlyle Hotel. I told you, he is safe."

"No, he's not. He's not at the Carlyle anymore. I was just there. He's gone." Schuyler told them what they had found—the television blaring, the half-eaten dinner. "I think he was the one who attacked me."

For a long moment, nothing was said. Charles looked at Schuyler wrathfully. "If what you are saying is true, we must find him. Immediately."

FORTY-ONE

*S*he was screaming, screaming so loudly, as if no one would ever hear her. It was the nightmare again—someone taking hold of her—squeezing the breath out of her—and nothing she could do to stop it—she was gagging—she was drowning—and then—fighting against the force that was holding her down, she struggled, trying to wake up, forcing herself to push herself out of bed—she had to open her eyes—she had to see—she saw.

She saw the two of them looking at her. Her parents. Her father was wearing his flannel robe over his pajamas, and her stepmother had a peignoir over a nightgown.

"Bliss, darling, are you all right?" her father asked. He was home from D.C. for the week.

"I had a nightmare," Bliss said, sitting upright and tossing the covers to the side. She put a hand up to her forehead, feeling the heat emanate from her skin. She was burning and feverish.

"Another one?" her stepmother asked.

"A bad one."

"It's all part of it, Bliss. Nothing to worry about," her father said cheerfully. "I remember when I was your age, I used to have awful ones. Comes with the territory. Blackouts too—when I was fifteen, a lot of times I'd wake up somewhere and have no idea how I got there, and no idea what happened." He shrugged. "Part of the transformation."

Bliss nodded, accepting the cold glass of water her stepmother proffered. She gulped greedily. Her father had mentioned that before, when she'd first told him about the time slips, her blackouts.

"I'm okay," she told them, although she felt so tired, like every muscle in her body was sore, as if she'd been pummeled and beaten up all over. She groaned.

They hovered over her anxiously.

"I'm all right. Really." Bliss managed a smile and took another huge gulp of water. "You guys go back to bed. I'm *fine*."

Her father kissed her on her forehead, and her mother patted her arm, and the two of them left the room.

She put the glass down on her bedside table. Then she remembered—Dylan.

After saying good-bye to Oliver and Schuyler at the Carlyle, she had met her family for a quick dinner at DB Bistro. Upon returning home, she had opened the door to her room, and Dylan was sitting on her bed, as if it was the most normal thing in the world. He'd used the key she'd lent him to get inside.

"Dylan!"

He was feverish and pale. He'd taken off his jacket and she saw that his T-shirt and jeans were torn. His dark hair was matted against his forehead. He looked spooked. Terrified. His eyes were haunted. He told her what happened—being questioned, and held, but not formally charged, how Charles Force had taken him to the hotel suite, and the whole time he was just thinking about how he missed her.

"But the thing is, I think I did do something," he said. His hands were shaking. "I think they were right. I think I killed Aggie. I'm not sure, but I think there's something wrong with me."

"Dylan—no. No way. You couldn't have," Bliss said.

"You don't understand," Dylan cried. "I'm a vampire. Like you, a Blue Blood."

Bliss just stared at him. It suddenly made sense. Of course he was one of them, she'd known it somehow, that was why she'd been drawn to him all along. Because he was just like her.

"But something's happening to me . . . I'm not sure, but I think I just tried to kill Schuyler . . . I saw her leave the hotel, and I followed her. I don't know why, it just came over me. I saw her on the street and I . . . I don't think it's the first time either."

"No," Bliss said, refusing to hear what he had to say. "Stop. You're not making sense." Why would he attack Schuyler? Unless he was . . . unless he'd become . . . unless he'd turned into a . . . She remembered that night after the photo shoot. Schuyler, staggering on the sidewalk, clutching the side of her neck . . .

"Listen," he said, standing up from the bed and putting his jacket back on. "You need to get out of here. They got me, and they're going to get you too. They want all of us. I only came back to warn you, but I can't stay. I don't think it's safe for you to be around me. But I wanted to tell you to be careful. I don't want them to get you. You have to protect yourself. You've got to believe me. *They're coming. . . .*"

Then everything went blank. That was all she remembered.

She had blacked out. She was in her skin and not in her skin. She slipped through time and went somewhere else. When she woke up, she was screaming, and her parents were standing above her bed.

Dylan had come to warn her—and now he was gone.

She felt a dull emptiness, an ache, deep in her bones, as if she had survived a beating. She walked to the bathroom and turned on the light. She gasped when she looked at herself in the mirror. There was a mark underneath the collar of her T-shirt. Had her parents not noticed? She pulled on the fabric to see it better. It was an ugly bruise. A dark purple swelling, as if someone had tried to strangle her. The skin was tender to her touch. What had happened? Where was Dylan?

She turned on the faucet to wash her face, when she noticed shards of pulverized glass on the bathroom floor. The room was cold. She turned toward the window. The curtains billowed from a draft. The top of the windowpane was shattered—and it was bulletproof glass—her father had had it installed when they moved in, even if they were on the highest floor of the building—thirty stories high.

Bliss picked her way carefully through the broken glass, when she noticed something strange. Next to the heater, a dark crumpled thing. She reached for it and pulled out Dylan's motorcycle jacket. Dylan never went anywhere without his jacket. It was like his second skin. It smelled like him—a little sour, like cigarettes and aftershave.

There was something different about it, though. She turned the jacket toward the light, and that's when she saw it. The lining was soaked with blood. Thick and wet. Heavy. There was so much blood. Oh God . . .

She was still holding the jacket when she noticed Jordan standing in front of the bathroom door. A small, silent form in cotton pajamas.

"You scared me. Ever think of knocking? You know you're not allowed in my room!" Bliss said.

Her younger sister looked at her as if she'd seen a ghost. "You're okay."

"Of course I am," Bliss snapped.

"I heard something—I heard—a deep voice . . ."

"Dylan. My boyfriend. He was here with me earlier."

"No, not the boy—another," Jordan said. She was shaking violently, and Bliss was surprised to find her sister near tears. She'd never seen Jordan act that way before.

Bliss, still holding the jacket, walked to her side and held her close. "What did you hear?" she asked, trying to soothe her trembling sister.

"There was a thump—like—something heavy dropping—then footsteps, out of your room—dragging something away—then you were screaming—I, I didn't know what to do—so I called Mom and Dad. . . ."

It all made sense now.

The broken window.

Someone had been there.

Someone else.

Or more likely, some*thing*.

And it had . . . oh God, Dylan . . . all the blood—there was so much blood on the jacket—how could anyone survive after losing so much blood? She felt a deep sense of grief. He was as good as dead. The creature had taken him.

It had returned, to finish the job—to get *her*—the swelling in her neck—she'd tried to fight it off—if Jordan hadn't heard, if her parents hadn't come. . . . She felt chills. The fine hair on her arms stood on end.

It was no nightmare—she'd been fighting it—it had been there, it was real. It had tried to kill her. What Dylan had tried to warn her about, what she and Oliver and Schuyler had discovered in the Repository. Croatan. A creature that preyed on vampires.

A Silver Blood.

FORTY-TWO

*T*he Forces dropped her off in front of her door. Schuyler was painfully embarrassed to think that she had accused Jack's father of being a Silver Blood. Even though she was still troubled by his cavalier attitude toward their return—almost as if it didn't bother him—almost as if he had expected it. But that couldn't be true. He was the Regis, their leader, a vampire by choice instead of sin. She had to trust him to know the right thing to do.

"Take it easy," Jack said, bidding her good-bye.

She nodded her thanks and exited from the car. Then she realized she had completely forgotten to ask why Charles was visiting her mother in the first place. Maybe her grandmother would know.

When Schuyler entered the house, she felt a strangeness in the air. The sitting room was as dark and shrouded as ever, but there was a feeling of menace. The umbrella stand had been knocked over, as if someone had run down the stairs in a hurry. The silence seemed ominous. Hattie was away on her week off, and her grandmother would be alone in the house. Schuyler quickened her pace up the stairs. She noticed one of the paintings hanging in the stairway was askew. Someone had definitely been in the house. Someone who did not belong there.

Dylan! What if Dylan had been here? Looking for her? To finish what he'd started? She felt a wild panic. Her grandmother's room was on the far end of the second landing. She threw the doors open and walked briskly inside, calling her name.

"Cordelia! Cordelia!"

There was a moan from the other side of the bed.

Schuyler ran toward the sound, frightened of what she would find. But she didn't scream when she saw Cordelia lying on the floor in a pool of her own blood—thick blue liquid surrounding her—it was almost as if she had known it would happen.

"Fought it off . . . but so powerful . . ." Cordelia whispered, opening her eyes to see Schuyler leaning over her.

"Who? Who did this to you?" Schuyler asked, helping Cordelia to a sitting position. "We need to get you to a hospital."

"No, no time." Cordelia argued, her voice barely louder than a croak. "Came for me. Croatan." She spit up blood.

"Who? Was it Dylan? Did you see?"

Cordelia shook her head. "I saw nothing. I was blinded momentarily. But it was young, powerful. I did not see its face. I held it off. It tried, but it wasn't able to take me or my memories. But this is the end of my cycle. You need to take me to Dr. Pat's. So they can take my blood. For the next Expression. Very important."

Schuyler nodded, tears in her eyes. "But what about you?"

"This cycle is ended for me. This is the last chance we will have to speak for a long time."

Schuyler told her quickly about what happened at the Carlyle, and what she'd learned from Charles Force about Dylan, how he'd been bitten, and turned, by a Silver Blood. How he had killed Aggie. "But he's missing. He escaped from the hotel room. Nobody knows where he is."

"He is most likely dead by now. They will kill him before he can reveal their secrets. Before the Blue Bloods can hold him again. It is as I always feared," Cordelia whispered. "The Silver Bloods are back . . . Only you can defeat them . . . Your mother was the strongest of us and you are her daughter. . . ."

"My mother?"

"Your mother was Gabrielle. Gabriel. One of the seven Archangels. Only two of them went voluntarily with the cursed, down to earth. To save us. She was the strongest. She was Michael's—that is—Charles Force's twin. His only love. It was her original sacrifice. He only followed out of his love for her. He gave up Paradise to be with her."

So that was why Charles visited her mother. Allegra was his sister. Which meant, he was her . . . uncle? The tangled Blue Blood family history was too complicated for Schuyler to make sense of it at the moment. Cordelia continued speaking. "They ruled together for thousands of years. In Egypt, pharaohs routinely married their sisters, as the emperors did in Rome. But in the modern world, the practice became increasingly proscribed, and so it became a hidden secret. Twins were still born in the same families, blood-bound to each other like I was to your grandfather; but through a change, one twin would assume the role of spouse, and the Red Bloods never noticed the transition. This way, fortunes were preserved in the same family for generations."

Schuyler thought of Mimi and Jack, of the strange and intimate bond between them.

"Charles and Allegra were blood-bound to each other for eternity. Until she met your father, that is. Your mother fell in love with Stephen. It was her doom. She renounced Charles. In his anger, Charles left the family. He took a new name and forsook the Van Alen legacy. When your father died, Allegra swore never to take another human familiar, to preserve their love. It is why she does not wake up. She exists between life and death. She refuses to take the Red Blood to keep her alive. Charles could help her, but chooses not to."

"My father was human?"

"Yes. You are the only one. You are a Half Blood. *Dimidium Cognatus*. You must take care. I have protected you as long as I could. There are those who will seek to destroy you."

"Who? Why?"

"It is said that the daughter of Gabrielle will bring us to the salvation we seek."

"Me? How?"

Cordelia coughed. She gripped Schuyler's arm tightly. "You must find your grandfather . . . my husband . . . Teddy . . . an Enmortal, a vampire who has kept the same physical shell for centuries. . . . He and I separated a long time ago. After we were banished from the Conclave, we agreed it was safer to separate . . . We did not trust the Wardens . . . We believed one of them harbored the Croatan . . . Teddy has been missing for centuries . . . You must search the Repository for his last known whereabouts . . . He can help you. Try Venice, I think. He was fond of Italy. He might have gone there. Only he knows how to defeat the Silver Bloods. You must find him and tell him what's happened."

"How will I know him?"

Cordelia smiled wanly. "He's written a lot of books. Most of the ones in the library are from his collection, or were written by him."

"Who was he? What was his name?"

"He has many names. You need them, you know, if

you're going to live for so long. But when we were together last he was going by Lawrence Winslow Van Alen. Comb the Piazza San Marco. And the Academy. Wait—Cipriani's is most likely. He did love his Bellinis. Tell him, tell him Cordelia sent you."

Schuyler nodded. She wept openly now. There were so many things yet to fathom—Charles/Michael, Allegra/Gabriel, her human father, her immortal grandfather. She certainly had a strange and varied family tree. Her status as a Half Blood. Who else knew? Did Oliver? Jack? And what did it mean? What did it mean that Gabrielle's daughter would bring the Blue Bloods to salvation? It was too much. It was too big a burden to shoulder. She wanted nothing more than for Cordelia to stop bleeding. How would she go on without her?

Even though she knew her grandmother would never really die—she was still leaving this world for the time being.

"Grandmother," she pleaded. "Stay."

"Take care of yourself, granddaughter," she said, reaching for Schuyler's hand. "*Facio Valiturus Fortis.*" Be strong and brave. With that final blessing, Cordelia Van Alen's spirit reverted to a passive state.

FORTY-THREE

The funeral was SRO—Standing Room Only. It was amazing how many people knew Cordelia Van Alen. St. Bartholemew's was packed, and on the seventh night of viewing, there were still hundreds of people who showed up to pay their respects. The governor, the mayor, the two senators from New York, and many other people came to pay homage. It was almost as crowded as Jackie O's funeral, Mimi thought.

Unlike at Aggie Carondolet's funeral, almost every person attending had worn white to Cordelia Van Alen's. Even her father had insisted that the family dress in ivory raiment for the occasion. Mimi had chosen a cloud-colored Behnaz Sarafpour dress. She noticed Schuyler Van Alen at the front of the receiving line, greeting everyone in a slim white dress, her hair held back by two white gardenias.

"Thank you for coming," she told the Forces, shaking their hands.

"We share your sorrow. She shall return," Charles Force said solemnly. He was wearing a suit the color of cream. Schuyler had kept the circumstances of her grandmother's death to herself. If there was really a Silver Blood in the Conclave, she felt it best not to reveal what had truly happened. Instead, she had told everyone that Cordelia had tired of the Expression and was looking forward to resting before the next cycle.

"We await for glad tidings," Schuyler said the traditional reply back. She had learned a lot in the past two months.

"*Vos Vadum Reverto*," Jack whispered, bowing to the coffin. *You Shall Return.*

Mimi gave Schuyler a quick nod. She found Bliss arriving through the side door with her family. Bliss was wearing a Sarafpour shift dress identical to Mimi's. The girl from Texas was learning, too.

"Hey, Bliss, maybe after the funeral we can go to a spa. I'm so sore from power yoga," Mimi said to her friend.

"Sure," Bliss said. "I'll wait for you after the service." She walked up to Schuyler, who was standing by herself by the magnificent platinum coffin.

"Sorry about your grandmother," Bliss said.

"Thank you," Schuyler said, her eyes downcast.

"What are you going to do now?"

Schuyler shrugged. In her will, Cordelia had declared Schuyler an emancipated minor, with Hattie and Julius as her guardians for now.

"I'll be okay."

"Good luck."

Schuyler watched Bliss walk away, huddled closely to Mimi. The day before, Bliss had told her about the other night, what had happened when she'd returned from the Caryle. How she'd found Dylan in her room, how he'd confessed. How she'd blacked out, and when she awoke, had discovered the broken glass, the bloodstained jacket.

"He was a vampire and now he's dead, Schuyler," Bliss said, tears in her eyes.

No—not dead. Worse than dead, Schuyler thought. Cordelia had told her that when the Silver Bloods drained the Blue Bloods, they took their souls, their memories, made them prisoner to their immortal consciousness forever.

"They took him, but they wanted me too," Bliss sobbed. "He only came back to warn me. They'd turned him into one of them, but he was fighting it. Now he's gone, and I'll never see him again."

Schuyler had hugged her close. "At least you're safe."

She felt heartsick for Bliss. She wanted her know that she would always be there for her. But the next day, it seemed the Texan girl had completely reverted to her old self. She refused to talk to Schuyler or Oliver about everything that happened, and gravitated back to her old circle—that is, next to Mimi Force.

Schuyler hoped that they would get a chance to become friends again. In her heart, she understood that Bliss was weak, but someday she would help her become strong. *Valiturus. Fortis.*

Oliver came over and placed a spray of white calla lilies on the coffin. He was wearing a dazzling three-piece white suit. His dark chestnut hair curled above the collar.

"We will miss her," he said, blessing himself.

"Thank you," she said, accepting a kiss on the cheek.

The service began, and the choir sang Cordelia's favorite hymn, "On Eagle's Wings." Schuyler sat in the front pew, her arms folded in her lap. Cordelia was gone. The only family she had ever truly known. She was alone in the world. Her mother, trapped in a sleeping death, and her grandfather lost, hiding somewhere.

Oliver, seated next to her, squeezed her hand in sympathy.

After the funeral, Jack Force walked over to Schuyler. He, too, was wearing a white suit, and it gleamed in the sun. They walked out of the church to busy Park Avenue, where it was just another Sunday in New York. Mothers and nannies pushing eight-hundred-dollar strollers toward the park, well-dressed residents out for a brisk fall stroll or an afternoon at a museum.

"Schuyler, could I have a sec?"

"Sure." She shrugged.

With his light hair and green eyes, Jack Force looked princely in his shining garb. He had the face of an angel. A face not unlike his father's.

"Speak," she told him.

"I'm sorry things went so weird between us. . . ." he said. "I . . . my life is not my own. . . . I have responsibilities to my family that . . . that preclude the kind of relationship that—"

"Jack, you don't need to explain," Schuyler said, cutting him off. She could guess about him and Mimi. Blood-bound to each other since the day of their creation.

"No?"

"You need to do what you need to do, and I need to do what I need to do."

He looked troubled. "What do you need to do?"

She thought about Dylan, about the sad-faced boy with the wicked sense of humor and the tarnished reputation. Her *friend*. He had been transformed into a monster. Used and then killed. She thought about what her grandmother had said about the Silver Bloods—they were wily, cunning, and duplicitous, and how Cordelia believed the most power-ful of them all was hiding among them, disguised as a Blue Blood. But no one wanted to believe in their existence, that there was a chance they had returned. Even if Aggie's death was real enough. And now Dylan's as well. Charles Force was determined to watch, wait, and do nothing. But Schuyler would not wait. There was nothing she could have done for Aggie, but she had to find out who had taken Dylan. She would hunt down the Silver Bloods. Avenge her friend.

"Don't make things any harder for yourself, Schuyler," Jack warned.

Schuyler only smiled. "Good-bye, Jack."

Oliver materialized suddenly. It was amazing how he always showed up right when Schuyler needed him the most.

"Schuyler? The car's waiting," he said.

She linked her arm in his and let him walk her to the car. She had Oliver. She would never be alone.

FORTY-FOUR

*T*he Stitched for Civilization billboard went up in Times Square, the biggest billboard the city had ever seen. The photograph was an unusual one: there was a tangle of two female bodies wearing only the jeans, but only one face was visible and looked toward the camera. Schuyler. Bliss's face was obscured by all her red hair.

Schuyler looked up at herself and laughed.

Oliver took a photo with his cell phone of Schuyler pointing to her billboard and giggling.

"You look good eighty feet high," he said.

Schuyler looked at the face on the billboard. Her mother's face. No, the face was her own. She looked like her mother but she had her father's eyes. She was a vampire, but part of her was human as well. She was proud of the photograph. Then she saw the billboard across from it.

It was an advertisement for Force News Network, FNN,

and the photograph was of Mimi Force wearing the channel's logo on a tight white T-shirt. FORCE NEWS. FAIR, JUST, AND FAST.

"Look," she said, pointing.

So Mimi had heard about the Stitched for Civilization campaign after all. And had tried to eclipse it by making herself a billboard too. No one was going to rule Times Square but her.

They walked past a newsstand and Oliver paid for the *Post*.

PREPPIE FOUND DEAD AT A PARTY. The headline blared.

Schuyler scrutinized the article. She knew the kid from The Committee. Landon Schlessinger was a Blue Blood. She was running out of time. The Silver Bloods had returned. They were back. They were here, in New York, hiding under false Blue Blood identities, infringing on their community, preying on the young, during the time when the Blue Bloods were the weakest. And the Blue Bloods would just let it happen.

But not anymore. She folded the newspaper and tucked it under her arm.

"Ollie, how do you feel about a weekend in Venice?" she asked.

A note on the text:

This is a work of fiction, but is set in a real place—New York City. However, I have taken some liberties. The American Society Mansion is inspired by The Americas Society mansion on Park Avenue and East Sixty-eighth Street. The Americas Society is devoted to promoting the understanding of the culture and politics of the Western Hemisphere (including South America), while my fictional American Society is devoted to the early colonial history of the United States of America.

True story: the Lost Colony of Roanoke was founded in 1587 and discovered to be missing in 1590, save for the word "Croatan" carved on a post.

Acknowledgments

Heartfelt thanks to the book's fairy godmothers—Brenda Bowen, Helen Perelman, and Elizabeth Rudnick, who gave me a ship and let me fly. Thank you to Colin Hosten, Elizabeth Clark, and everyone at Hyperion for believing in this book. Thanks to Richard Abate, Kate Lee, Josie Freedman, and James Gregorio and Karen Kenyon at ICM for their fantastic support.

Hugs and kisses to the amazing DLCs and Johnstons: Mom—thank you for being at every reading and for always being there for me; Aina, Steve, Nico, and Chito—we are family, and we can boogie, too (especially Nicholas!); Dad J and Mom J—thank you for all your support and for buying all those books; John, Anji, Alex, Tim, Rob, Jenn, Val, and the one on the way—we are family and we can mosh pit, too! Thanks to all the extended family, especially the Torres, the Gaisanos, the Ongs, the Izumis, and the de la Cruzes.

Many thanks to the LA and NY support groups: Tristan Ashby, Jennie Kim, Kim DeMarco, Gabriel Sandoval, Tom Dolby, Tyler Rollins, Jason Lundy, Andy Goffe, Jeff Levin, Peter Edmonston, Mark Hidgen, Caroline Suh, Doug Meehan, Thad Sheely, Gabby Sheely, Mindy Wilson, Ji Gilbreth, Catherine Hong, Yumi Kobayashi, Peter Sluszka, Ruth Basloe, Andrey Slivka, Alice Carmona, Michael Casey, Karen Robinovitz, Kate Roche, John Fox, Carol Fox, Karlo Pastrovic, Gabriel de Guzman, Edgar Papazian, Michelle Lenzi, Matt Paco, Fitz Mangubat, Taylor Hsiao, Arisa Chen, Katie Davis, Tina Hay, Diva Gittel, Liz Craft, Adam Fierro, Anna David, MaryClare Williams, Alexandra Jacobs, Nicole Cannon, Ian Kornbluth, Brent Bryan, Nora Gordon, Matthias Kohlemainen, Juliet Gray, Karen Page, Andrew Dornenburg, Sara Shandler, Emily Thomas, Jennifer Zatorski, Abby McAden, Allison Dickens, Jared Paul Stern, Lisa Marsh, Andrew Stone, Ben Widdicombe, Norah Lawlor, and Katie Murphy.

Thanks also to our little Peapod, who we will miss forever.

MELISSA DE LA CRUZ is the author of many books for teens and adults, including *The Au Pairs* and its sequel, *Skinny-Dipping*. *The Au Pairs* has been published in nine countries. She is also the author of the novels *Cat's Meow* and *Fresh Off the Boat*, and co-authored the tongue-in-chic handbooks *The Fashionista Files: Adventures in Four-Inch Heels and Faux-Pas* and *How to Become Famous in Two Weeks or Less*.

Melissa has appeared as an expert on style, trends, and fame for CNN and E! Entertainment Television and has written for *Glamour, Marie Claire, Harper's Bazaar, Allure, Teen Vogue, Cosmopolitan, CosmoGirl!* and *The New York Times*. She is a graduate of Columbia University. Melissa divides her time between New York City and Los Angeles, where she lives with her husband. She is currently working on several new books, including several sequels to *Blue Bloods*. Visit her Web site, Melissa-delacruz.com, for more information.